SONATA

SKYE WARREN

Who is Samantha Brooks without her violin? Fear lives in the silent spaces. Love does, too. There's a battle being waged in her heart, and Liam North is determined to win. He'll use every weapon in his arsenal. His body. His heart. Except the spotlight puts her in the crosshairs of dangerous men.

Samantha fights to compose her own ending, even as the final notes rise to a heartbreaking crescendo.

SONATA is the third and final book in the explosive trilogy with Samantha Brooks and Liam North. It should be read after OVERTURE and CONCERTO.

CHAPTER ONE

"The music is not in the notes, but in the silence between."
– Wolfgang Amadeus Mozart

SAMANTHA

THE SCENT OF ripe orange mixes with brine. Pungent fresh flowers sharpen the calming pile of handmade lavender soap. Farmers and fishermen fill the stalls as the dawn's light turns from pale to yellow. I stroll through the market, my canvas bag heavy with peaches.

In one stall a man works rope into braids through his gnarled fingers. Rugs and baskets line the stall. Shells form designs through the hemp. A row of sand dollars and starfish line the wood countertop. I pick up a large conch shell and put it to my ear. Ocean sounds shimmer from the space. It's the only music I've had since we came here to hide. It feels like a Band-Aid on a gaping wound—not nearly enough to staunch the bleeding.

"Ten euros," the man says in a heavy accent.

It's more than a good price. It's low. If we were a few miles south, with the touristy hotels and casinos, it would go for five times that much. I set the shell back down on the scarred wood. It's not the price that stops me, but the possession. I can keep it in the flat, but then what? Should I cart it around in my suitcase if we move once again? I've been reduced to a nomadic existence, the same as my childhood.

"You came back," the woman at the baker's stall says in French. I'm learning bits and pieces. Enough to stumble my way through a purchase, almost definitely paying more than I should.

On the other hand, living among people who speak a foreign language makes me appreciate the words we say with our bodies, our hands, our eyes. The urgency of desperation, the casual cruelty of indifference. Every glance tells a story. The baker's, with her knowing eyes, speaks of a port in the storm. *Rest here, where you're not in danger, even if you're not among friends.*

"How long are you here?" she asks.

My mind works through the words. Mastery in music is supposed to make learning languages easy, but that's never been true for me. Language has too many secrets. It's more about obscuring than sharing. With music there's no place to hide, assuming you even wanted to. That's the magic of it. It's also the dark side. People reveal more than they know.

"A few weeks," I say, reciting my story in broken French. A small grimace. "As long as I can before my dad cuts off my credit card. I don't want to tell him about flunking Organic Biology."

She nods, full of conspiratorial approval. The town outside Nantes is too small to blend in. So we don't bother trying. Instead I fulfill the stereotype of the American girl from a wealthy family, following her dreams for a foolhardy summer before I return to settle down to a life of eco-SUVs and tennis shorts. My terrible French suits the role perfectly.

Baguettes and loaves pile on top of each other in an elegant sprawl. A tin cake stand features a few pastries. It feels decadent to even admire them. Strawberry and basil scones. Chocolate chili pepper tart. My stomach tightens into a knot. I point to a plain baguette. It will go with plain eggs and plain yogurt. It suits the plain walls of our rented flat.

"*Deux*," I say, pulling euros from my pocket.

She makes change efficiently, and I grasp the crust with my bare hands, stacking them in my canvas bag. I wave my thanks and lick the crumbs from my fingertips. There's no wax paper or rolls of plastic bags like in a regular grocery store. Everything here is drenched in sunshine. It might be the eighteenth century, the lanes only wide enough for a horse and buggy, the cobblestones uneven beneath my sandals. A market has been here every Sunday for centuries. Only the stand at the end, with its secondhand iPhones and bootleg Fortnite CDs, proves we're still in modern times.

I break from the crowd, turning towards home. A shadow follows mine.

It's only there for a heartbeat. I might have imagined it. Then the sun outlines my head and shoulders as if I'm truly alone. *I'm not.* My pulse beats a warning drum. I pull the bag close to me and speed up, keeping my head down. Three steps. Four. Five.

Around a corner. I break into a run, the bag slamming against my hip, the peaches bruised beneath the canvas. I take a different way home every time I visit the market. Terrible lessons. They keep me alive.

This way pulls me through a narrow alley with clotheslines hanging faded sheets. My flying leg knock against a box that starts to emit the mew of kittens and the hiss of their mama. It's almost enough to make me stop. They probably know better how to survive in this world than I do.

My lungs burn, but I run faster than before—determined. For what reason, I don't know. I'm less sure as the days go on, less certain of anything. Not even music can save me.

When I reach Rue des Coquilles I slow to a casual walk, forcing myself not to breathe hard and give myself away. Nameless faces bustle past me. That's what I've become: nameless. I tuck my head against my chin, warding off the cold. There's only a pleasant breeze on the sea-swept air. The chill comes from inside me.

That's how I enter the small house that serves as our temporary jail. I smell her acidic orange perfume before I see her. Madame Tissot appears at the bottom of the staircase as if she's been waiting for me. Maybe she has.

"You're leaking," she says by way of greeting.

I glance down, where an egg yolk dangles obscenely from the corner of my tote bag. "Shoot. I'd better take this upstairs."

Madame Tissot isn't French by birth. She grew up in Colorado before she fell in love with a Mr. Tissot, who brought her here before he inconveniently died in a car crash while visiting his whore. Her words. Not mine. She does not seem inclined to let me pass. "Did you get hit by a bike?"

It's the way Mr. Tissot went. A small swipe from the handle of a motorbike in a too-narrow lane. He spun around only to slam his head into the concrete ground. "No, but I should get upstairs and salvage what's left of the groceries."

She doesn't move. Liam would never get caught in a conversion he didn't want. He managed to rent the apartment while sharing absolutely nothing about himself.

Meanwhile I get trapped every time I walk out the door.

Madame Tissot leans close enough that I smell her stale coffee from this morning. "You don't need to bother with groceries. Meals are included in your rent."

The weekly payment barely covers the two-bedroom apartment, much less food. I realized why the first morning I went down for breakfast. Sitting at the dining table meant talking. It's Madame Tissot's sad little social circle. I feel bad for her, lonely in this leftover house, but not enough to go back.

I make a vague gesture. "Oh, you know. It's no trouble."

Realization dawns on her face. "And you

probably want privacy."

"It's not like that," I say, too quickly. Because it *is* like that. We need privacy for hiding and planning. Not for sex, the way the twinkle in her eyes implied. "We aren't together."

She frowns, and belatedly I realize I'm supposed to be a college student on a break. "He's… my father," I mutter. "He's kind of pissed at me, but we're working it out."

"Ahhh, I see." The lights in her dark eyes shift, showing a decided feminine interest in the handsome, brooding tenant who's no longer taken. "He does not understand your wish for independence?"

I don't know why it feels so strange to pretend Liam's my father. It fits the cover story—and has the added benefit of being mostly true. That's all we are right now. All we'll ever be. The fact that I thought we'd be more… "No, he doesn't understand."

"You're throwing away your future," she says on a fake male voice. "You don't know enough about the world to make these decisions. I know what's best for you."

"Exactly," I say, surprised that the complaints of a father with an errant sorority girl so closely match my real situation. Apparently being a violin prodigy does not spare me the ordinary problems. The thought brings me a strange comfort. I've always wanted to be normal.

"Of course, the irony. How can you learn about the world unless you fail?"

My heart stops at the word *fail*. Is that what I've done? There's no F on my transcript. No incomplete coursework sitting at some university, the way she thinks. Instead there's a global tour deserted. A career as a professional violinist— abandoned.

I mumble some incoherent goodbye before starting up the stairs. They creak and moan, announcing my arrival to the man on the other side. The one who followed me home.

Right after the shooting in New York City, I was more worried about the bullet in Liam's lung. We were worried about making sure we weren't followed, that we retreated deep enough to be safe. It was only later that I realized Liam's angry with me. No, that's not the right word. He's furious with me. A soul-deep rage that I can't understand or breach. I've never seen his anger before, not really. I wasn't the kind of teenager to stay out past curfew or spend too much at the mall. Even if I had, he'd been too stoic to let much show. This is different. It simmers near the surface whenever we're in the same room, scalding me without a single touch.

LIAM

THE ROOF IS occupied. I waited fifteen minutes after Samantha left for the market before climbing the fire escape. Josh North leans against a hollow metal air vent, black sunglasses blocking his eyes, so like my own. "Fancy meeting you here," he says.

My chest feels tight—surprise, relief, guilt. Seeing one of my brothers has the predictable reaction. Feelings that I'd rather not feel. I give him a curt nod and leap to the next rooftop, landing soft on my feet even though it makes my side ache.

Air brushes my side. Josh lands beside me, soundless. "Should you be doing that?"

"Probably not."

We continue moving over the rooftops, separating once around the steeple of a medieval church. Our movements are careful enough that we could be on a mission together. It's natural to treat it that way. We lived under threat long before we enlisted.

I stop at the building beside the marketplace.

A hundred people mill between stalls. The air is filled with shouts from farmers and fishermen. Down the alleyway boys play soccer on the cobblestone. Samantha bargains at a fruit stand, looking fresh and pure in a white lace top and flowing beige skirt.

Only when I see her can I breathe again. "Why are you here?" I ask the question without turning. I can feel his presence beside me. Of course he would have found me. It isn't an accident that I brought Samantha here to recover. Russia is where our story began, but France—this is where we'll end.

"I found the file you wanted."

That makes me look at him. "You were supposed to use the drop box. Fine. What did it say?"

"It's empty. Almost empty. A few pages of useless bullshit."

"Christ." That means the corruption in the US government goes higher than we suspected. Most of our missions were classified. We know the dark side of politics. The foreign leader who dies of natural causes in another country. The militia with leaking intelligence. That was our job before we left service and started North Security.

Samantha's father was a diplomat. His records would have the highest clearance, but Josh is owed enough favors from the people in the State Department to get it.

Information might be redacted or blacked out, but if it's missing entirely? That means someone at a very high level has tampered with official documents.

That means treason.

Josh crouches low on the rooftop, running his hands through a smattering of pebbles and detritus on the edge. Three indents mark the soft concrete underneath. He gives a low laugh. "You scoped out a five-mile radius, didn't you? Paranoid motherfucker."

"It doesn't matter. We can't stay here forever."

"Can't you? Maybe you can buy a little cottage on the beach. She can weave baskets while you do whatever the fuck it is that men do around here. Get a boat. Fish."

"Samantha is a violinist."

"She hasn't played in weeks. Maybe—"

"Samantha is a violinist."

He looks away. I know he doesn't agree with the way I handle her. That makes us even. I don't agree with the way he handles a goddamn thing. "Whether she plays again or not, you don't need to follow her around. You definitely don't need to jump in front of another goddamn bullet."

"Then we'd better make sure there isn't another one." Because there's no way I'd ever let one touch her pale, soft skin. There are things I won't do when it comes to her. Leave her. I won't leave her. I'm feeling the sand run through my fingers. We're running out of time.

CHAPTER TWO

A study examined the deaths of artists and determined that a musician's lifespan averages 25 years shorter than the general U.S. population.

LIAM

I FORCE MYSELF to study the communication report, but stars blink in front of my eyes. Pain. Low blood pressure. Lack of oxygen. I catalog the physical responses without indulging in emotion. I've taken bullets before, but never one that tore this particular path through vital organs. Three months later, and I can barely manage to stand for an hour at a time.

Creaks on the stairs bring Samantha closer. It used to be a kind of peace, having her nearby, listening to her play in the room next to my office. The only peace I'd ever found. Now it's gone. Her approach spikes my heartbeat. Resentment ripples inside me. I have to force it back, behind a bland façade.

She opens the door, her expression determinedly cheerful. "There you are. I'm going to make sunny side up this morning. And there's some fresh baguettes to dip the yolk."

Sunshine. That's what she looks like. Bright enough to blind me.

I glance down at the yolk in question, which bobs precariously near the floor. Even if there are unharmed eggs in the bag, I'll probably be served that specific one, replete with dirt and shell, as punishment for making her run. I have to know, though. Have to know that she can spot a tail and lose it.

Or maybe I'm punishing her for choosing this life. The running. The hiding. This is what she picked instead of being in the goddamn spotlight. *For you,* a low voice murmurs. It sounds like my father. She gave it up to keep me safe, the tour canceled, tickets refunded by the time I could stand. I'm the reason she no longer has a bright future, and it's killing me worse than that bullet.

"I already ate," I say, pushing my gaze back to the report. It took the Red Team two weeks to put this intel together, and I can't even focus on it.

A sharp intake of breath as she sees the tray, complete with an omelet and orange juice and sprigs of fresh lavender. "How did you get

Madame Tissot to agree to this?"

"I didn't." It was the cook I bribed. First with money. Then, when the cook deduced my skillset and arsenal from the maid, she asked for a different payment. Her sister's husband used his fist to do the talking. And so one night, while Samantha slept in the little twin bed with lace-trimmed sheets, I climbed onto the roof and walked the city. A single bullet.

That's all it takes to end a life.

Part of me wants to tell Samantha. The perverse part of me.

That's who you gave up your career for—someone with blood on his hands. A murderer. I killed someone for a goddamn omelet. So that you could have breakfast sent up. And you know what? I'm not even sorry. I'd do it again. Do you want dinner, too? Surely there's some other sorry soul who needs to sleep.

Except if I do that, she'll look at me with horror in her soulful eyes.

I'm not ready for that.

She turns to the sink at the small countertop, carefully emptying the bag and rinsing her purchases. Soaking the bottom of the tote bag to clean the egg away. It's startlingly domestic, her bare feet on the laminate, the stream of water running over her fingers.

I stand to join her and I'm aware of a warm trickle down my side. The wound must have opened. It probably happened on that last jump between buildings. My breath catches. Barely a movement of molecules in the air. She hears it, of course.

Her dark eyes flash with something like anger. It reminds me that I'm not the only one pissed off about this situation. Neither of us knows where to put these feelings. She's the obedient one, the good girl. I'm the one full of restraint and ignoble desires. Who are we if not those old people? Both of us locked in four hundred square feet, a prison of our own making.

"You're supposed to rest," she says, her voice moderated enough to be bland. She doesn't say, *you're doing this to hurt me,* but the words drift in the air between us.

I'm not doing this to hurt her. I'm doing this to hurt myself, and it's just her terrible luck that she's grown to care about someone like me. "And you're supposed to stay in the apartment."

She's not listening to me. Instead she's rummaging in the box that contains our first aid materials. It takes her too long to sort through the bandages and lotions. Long enough to get her emotions under control. "Take off your shirt."

My body has the predictable response to those words, even though she says them cold enough to freeze any normal man. I'm not a normal man. She could hate me, probably *does* hate me, and I'd still want inside her so bad it aches. I pull the blood-stained T-shirt over my head. Bright red spreads over a white bandage. "You don't have to look at it," I say, my voice low. She's inches away from me now, head bent so I can't see her expression.

"Stay still." Gentle hands remove the bandage. She doesn't flinch at the way the skin has blackened around the edges of the wound. I know I'm not taking care of it well enough. I'd tear down a soldier under my command who let it fester. Your body is your most important weapon, I'd say. You wouldn't leave your gun outside to rust, would you? Part of me wants this wound—a physical manifestation of fear, a reminder of how close I came to losing her.

Antiseptic sharpens the air. She holds a dry washcloth beneath the wound. Then she tips the bottle of rubbing alcohol towards my abs, letting the burn wash over me.

Pain blinds me, flashing white hot behind my eyes.

I hiss a breath that turns into an unsteady laugh. Usually I dampen the washcloth with alcohol and apply it that way. Instead she's using it to catch the excess. She wanted to hurt me, and damned if I don't want to applaud her for it. "Looks like the kitten grew claws."

Her only response to my taunt is to keep pouring. She must want to empty the whole bottle. Some of the alcohol seeps through the washcloth, cool against the denim of my jeans. Sharp agony lances my side, as if it's pulling from deep inside me—my gut, my balls. Every part of me tight and hard.

I grasp her wrist to make her stop. The bottle falls, landing on the hardwood floor with a hollow sound, a swell of alcohol from its mouth. Finally, *finally,* she looks up at me.

Her eyes glisten with tears. My heart stops. She's crying. For me?

"I'm not worth the tears. Find something else to cry about. Someone who didn't have one foot in hell before he even saw you, sweetheart." I'm still holding her wrist, and I can't make myself let go. Now that I'm touching her soft skin, now that I'm feeling her pulse in my palm—it feels like gulping down air after an eternity spent underwater. Salt breeze touches my lips. The same salt that touches hers.

"Stop it." Tear tracks glisten on her cheeks, but she doesn't sound sad. She sounds furious. "You want to kill yourself? Then do it, but don't you dare do it protecting me, understand?"

I drag her close—close enough that I feel her body heat. Another centimeter and I'll seep fresh blood onto her white lace shirt. "So I'm not allowed to make sacrifices, but you are?"

"That's different."

"Do you dream about it?" I search her eyes for the grief she must feel, but I find only heat and resentment. She doesn't want to want me. That makes two of us. I dip my mouth close to hers. "The violin? The shape of it in your hands? The scent?"

"No."

I walk her back toward the wall, empty between two open windows, one of which I used to enter the apartment moments before she arrived. "Little liar. You probably lie awake at night wanting it, moving your hands beneath the sheets to the music in your head. It doesn't give you a moment of rest, does it?"

She shakes her head, slow and melodic, her gaze never leaving mine. "I'm fine." Her whisper breaks, because she's lying to me. "I don't need the violin."

"Such a brave girl," I murmur, pulling her flush against me. The heat makes me groan. The pain makes it sweeter. "You gave up your violin for me. Except you know I would never approve of that. I'd never have let you do it if I were conscious."

Her lower lip trembles. "I know you're mad about that, but—"

"Mad? Yes, that seems to be something we missed during our days of guardian and ward. The part where you break the rules and I have to punish you. Should I send you to bed without dinner?"

"But you have to agree it was the safest thing to do."

"Maybe I should turn you over my knee and spank you."

That takes her aback. "You wouldn't dare."

She should know better than to tempt me. I drop my head. Her lips cushion my own. Her scent invades me, climbing so deep it'll never leave.

My palm cups her head, cradling her, turning her so I can slip my tongue between her lips. Her body stiffens. She's thinking of pushing me away.

I move my other hand to her back, tucking

her close.

After a moment, she melts into me.

She tastes like sunshine and melancholy and a sweet endless guilt that I never want to relinquish. I sip on her sigh of pleasure, drunk with it.

SAMANTHA

IT'S THE FIRST time he's touched me in passion since the shooting. The first time I've touched him back for the pleasure of it. There's something darker about this pleasure. An undercurrent of anger that tightens his muscles. It isn't only lust that moves us now. It's something more primal.

The same thing that makes my finger move beneath the sheets at night.

How did he know that? Why did he say it? For the same reason I poured that alcohol on him. To hurt him. To heal him. The two purposes tangle together, opposite and equal.

"You don't get to punish me anymore, Liam."

"Don't I?" He's talking about more than a guardian. He's talking about the way a man can punish the woman who loves him—the way he's held me at arm's length has hurt me more than a spanking.

"Will you never forgive me for giving up the

violin?"

"I'll forgive you when you pick it up again."

My eyes narrow. "It's wrong of you to force me this way. It should be my choice."

His hand lifts mine in a courtly manner, almost as if he's going to kiss it. Then he examines my hand. Green eyes weigh their worth. My stomach churns. He dips his head. His lips press to the pad of my thumb. Not a smooth surface of skin. I have calluses from playing for hours. I've bled for my instrument. It still feels like I'm bleeding.

"I can't make you play again." He presses a kiss to my forefinger. "And you can't make me heal. So we arrive at this impasse, little prodigy. How will it end?"

"You could end it."

That earns me a grim smile. It kisses the point of my middle finger, where the calluses are the hardest. The raised skin should be too hardened to feel his lips, his breath. His tongue. "Why would I want to do that? Maybe I enjoy being in this prison with you."

"Enjoy it? You don't even touch me. You don't kiss me." My voice breaks at the end, and I can no longer pretend it doesn't make my heart shatter every time he looks at me in that remote way.

His lips press against my index finger. "I'm kissing you now."

"That's not—" He sucks my pinky finger into his mouth, his tongue moving over the tip in a way that's more explicit than if our bodies were naked. A shudder runs through me. The air shimmers with long-suppressed desire. "That's not what I meant."

"No?" He bites down on the plump of my palm, his teeth scraping against my skin, the sharp contact sensual in a base, animalistic way. I want his mouth in other places. I want him everywhere.

I squeeze my eyes shut, trying to force down the turmoil far enough so I can think. What did he ask me? *How will it end?* "Josh is looking for the people who funded my father."

A nip on my wrist. The pain makes my eyes fly open. Liam shakes his head slowly, almost sadly. "He's not going to find them. You're the only one who can do that."

Shock leaves me breathless. Or maybe that's the way his mouth skims my forearm. "How am I supposed to do that? By being your bait? That means more people shooting at us?"

"Are you worried I won't protect you this time?"

"You can't make me go!" Except the words don't feel sure, not when he's looming over me, not when my back's against the wall. He's the physical manifestation of power. He's the bow against the strings; I'm the music he makes. "You aren't even healed yet. You aren't—"

"We're going to Paris."

Paris. The city of love. We aren't going there for anything so romantic. It's also the city of light. If we're in hiding here by the sea, that will be our stage. "She thinks you're my father. Madame Tissot. She thinks I'm your daughter."

He doesn't flinch. He's too solid for that, but I feel the flicker in his soul. The guilt a man like him should never be allowed to have. The Achilles heel. Me. "You'll play the violin again. You'll play for me, Samantha. As long as I want. Forever. Understand?"

Something in me trembles at the word. *Forever.* "No."

"Yes," he says, hot against my inner wrist. It feels like I'm branded by him, as if he signed this devil's bargain with a breath. "I'll keep you with me, even if it fucking kills me. It just might, Samantha."

"What if I don't come with you? What if I refuse?"

"I may not spank you, little prodigy, but I won't have any problem picking you up and walking you down the road until we get to Paris."

Acid churns in my stomach. I want for this nightmare to end, but not if it means putting Liam in danger again. Not if it means playing the violin on stage again. My whole being shies away from that thought, like a night creature from the light. It's like I've become afraid of the bow. Afraid of the music. As if they've become gunshots. "Why does it matter so much to you if I play? Is that all I am to you? A machine to produce music?"

"A machine?" He licks the point of my pulse. "No. You're afraid. They wanted you to be afraid. That's why you sent your violin away. I'm going to get it back for you."

A quiver in my stomach. It might be too late already. I'm not the girl who stood on that stage in Carnegie Hall. Liam North presses an open-mouthed kiss to my hand—an ordinary hand. It used to play the violin with enough skill to rival anyone alive.

Now it's useless, useless, useless. "No."

"I'm not going to touch you until you play the violin again."

Surprise steals my voice. "Excuse me?"

It's annoying that he's being so high-handed but all I can think about is the pressure between my legs. I *want* him to touch me, and he knows that.

"Play the violin, and you can come."

"You can't be serious."

"I'm always serious."

My skin feels tight with arousal. "You're really going to leave me like this?"

"Yes. Although you don't have to wait for me to help you." He pushes it down, beneath the loose waistband of my linen skirt. "Touch yourself."

"Now?" Sunlight filters through the pale curtains. Arousal thrums through my body. He kissed my hand in the most sexual way, but that was different. That was... passive. I could accept what he did to me. This makes me a participant. From the gleam in his green eyes, he wants to see it. This isn't only about the violin.

"Yes. Now. Play a song for those clever little fingers. The way they move beneath the sheets. The way they hold the strings against the board."

A flush heats my cheeks. "You don't mean that."

"Of course I do. You haven't been practicing, have you? You need discipline. It's my job to give you that. We'll start now. Today. Practice on your pretty little pussy." As if to punctuate his command, he nudges my hand farther down my skirt. Private curls touch my fingertips. What am I thinking? Nothing, nothing. When he gives me an order, I'm trained to obey. I may not be the girl who performed at Carnegie Hall, but some things haven't changed.

I cup my sex beneath my panties, startled to find myself wet. It's one thing to be turned on. Another thing to be drenched when all he's done is kiss my hand. The same hand that brushes my clit. It's almost like he's kissing me there. Almost, but not quite. It would change everything, for him to really kneel in front of me. For him to touch me in this place. Oh, but I can touch myself. He watches my hand move beneath the free-flowing linen, his green eyes dark, his jaw clenched. It's a form of power, performing for him, even though I'm small and defenseless against him. Maybe that's what he wanted me to feel. Maybe that's what he wanted to remind me about playing the violin.

Or maybe he just wanted to see me climax.

His eyelids are heavy now. His lips a grim line on his harsh face. "Play the song you composed, little prodigy. I'll know if you don't."

"How?" I demand, the word almost voiceless. My fingers already do what he wants. "There isn't a bow. There aren't any strings. You can't hear anything."

"I'll know." He's implacable. Enough that my fingers form the positions, brushing my clit and then moving away. Brushing my clit and then moving away.

My breath catches. "Don't make me do this alone."

He's standing a foot away from me, half-naked and bleeding—but somehow coated in armor. I can't touch him. "You're always alone when you play," he says softly, almost sadly. "I'm the audience. The only thing I get to do is watch."

Stricken, I try to pull my hand away. He really is punishing me.

He holds my hand between my legs, implaca-ble, merciless. "Play the notes, Samantha."

A sob escapes. "You won't kiss me. You won't."

Emerald eyes show no mercy. He watches the fabric move as my hand plays, the notes pitch perfect, the music halted and strained on every breath. I come in a harsh pulse that's almost painful, and he does kiss me then—not on my lips. He brushes his lips on my forehead, a balm and an indictment all the same. I'm alone in the tight little orgasm, muscles clenched hard enough it feels like I'm crying.

CHAPTER THREE

Bach and Handel were born in the same year and only lived 80 miles apart, but they never met.

LIAM

THE FRENCH COUNTRYSIDE rushes past in a blur of greens and browns, an impressionist painting come to life on a speeding train. The server pushes a steaming cup of coffee across the counter.

Black. I take a sip. Not nearly strong enough, but it will have to do.

With habit borne of necessity I scan the surroundings: a man in a suit, a family with a crying baby, an older woman sitting alone reading a book.

Each person analyzed for risk and stored in my memory.

I study the menu for something to order Samantha. San Pellegrino. Perrier. She probably prefers tea, but she already had two cups this morning. Any more than that and she'll get jittery.

Christ. I'm thinking like her guardian again. Will I always try to take care of her? She isn't my ward any longer. Thank fuck, because I still remember the look of ecstasy on her face. I want to press her into the seat, to spread her legs and kneel in front of her, to make her cry out over the rhythmic thump of the train. "Earl Grey."

The French were never particularly fond of tea. Even cafes only have machines to make coffee, which are never quite enough for tea. Which means a train car definitely isn't equipped. The tea bag bobs at the top at the water, which isn't hot enough to sink it. I take a spoon and push it down so the leaves will soak.

First class isn't especially luxurious on a train, but it does mean our box is almost empty. I return to the seat opposite Samantha, who's on the phone. She gives me a weak smile in thanks. The sip of steaming liquid makes her eyes close in pleasure. My body tightens, and I look away.

"Something small." She gives a small, self-effacing laugh. "I'm sure that's all you can find for me right now. I really am sorry for the way I disappeared on you."

Her agent, then. I raise my eyebrow, which she pretends not to see. I hadn't told her to set up a performance, but it's a natural next step if we're going to use her as bait. She could probably be great at military strategy with that natural intelligence. The cryptographers would have a field day with her memory. Of course I'd put her underground for good before I'd let that touch her.

She's beauty in a world of violence. Without music, there's no point fighting a war.

A notch forms between her brows. "But Harry March isn't touring anymore. Why does the record label want to start it back up? Who's going to be the headliner?"

I know the answer before the agent says it. Samantha Brooks. She's always been the headliner. She didn't have the fanbase that Harry March did at the beginning of the tour… but she always had the talent. She always had the star power. Thanks to the successful North American run of the tour, she also has a following now. The drama of the shooting at Carnegie Hall only increased her celebrity. Every day the North Security servers sort through hundreds of press mentions. The important ones filter through Jameson, our resident analysis and information aficionado, who passes on the top bits to me.

Samantha blinks, clearly stunned. "I can't

carry an entire show."

Of course she can. Though she won't have to. There will always be an orchestra behind a soloist. Probably the gymnasts from the prior show. They might be able to find some European musician to join, but it will be Samantha's stage. It always has been.

Whatever her agent says makes her suck in a breath. "I played there once."

My mind begins working through the venues she played as a child prodigy. Those performances ended abruptly when her father died. When I got custody of her. That was a decision that many people would criticize, but I've never regretted it. She needed school and friends her age. She needed some semblance of an ordinary childhood after a nuclear wasteland.

Her talent is rare and powerful, but it doesn't define her.

"No," she says, sounding faint. "We're already heading to Paris."

The venue is in Paris? Then it must be the Palais Garnier. That's the only one she played as a child. An important opera house that should give an even greater boost to the tour's re-opening. It's also the perfect setting to lay a trap. My stomach tightens.

I don't want to use her as bait, but we've run out of options.

She promises to look for an email from her agent and ends the call. Her expression isn't overjoyed the way some musicians might be. Neither does she look nervous at the prospect of having thousands of theatergoers watching her play. Instead she looks pensive. Maybe even sad.

"I won't let you get hurt." The wound in my chest aches, as if to emphasize the lengths I'll go to keep her from harm. The bullet was meant for her. I would take a hundred of them.

A shadow passes over her face. "You may not have a choice."

Because I might not be able to protect her. New York City was too close. Fear churns my stomach. If I had been one second later crossing that stage… "*Samantha.*"

Her eyes search mine. "Don't feel guilty. That's not what I want from you."

"Then what is it you want?"

"Love," she whispers.

I try not to flinch. And fail. Because the one thing she wants is the thing I can't give her. Not the way she wants it. "I do."

"You love me as a daughter. As a guardian does a ward."

Frustration burns all the way down. "Does it matter the way I love you?"

"Yes."

A low growl. "Maybe I love you the way you want. How the hell would I know the difference? I'm not someone who was made to understand love. All I know is that I want you. I know the taste of you in my sleep."

"Look me in the eyes. Say, *I love you, Samantha Brooks.*"

Fuck. She doesn't know what she's asking for. Or maybe she does. It's like the bottle of rubbing alcohol pouring over an open wound. "Love is a word. It's a weakness. I protect you. That's all that matters."

"What's so wrong with loving someone?"

Because you're going to leave. It's something I could never explain to her. It's something she wouldn't understand. A bone-deep certainty. "This isn't the time or the place."

Even as I say the words, someone enters.

The heavy breath of the train mutes the sound of the sliding door and the steps of this woman. She might be passing through, except the only thing past us is more empty first-class cars. My mind catalogs anything noteworthy about her:

1) She was in the dining car when I got our

drinks

2) She holds a canvas bag from a bookstore in Paris

3) Now that I see her face, she looks vaguely familiar.

Other people might be inclined to discount her as a threat due to her age. Old women aren't usually seen as dangerous. Sometimes appearances are deceiving. I've seen children detonate bombs. I've seen old women smuggle cocaine. There is no one I would not consider protecting against.

Samantha offers a small smile. "When is the time? Where is the place?"

"Not a goddamn train," I manage to growl, even as my eyesight narrows. It's something that happens in battle. My heartbeat slows, so that my finger can pull the trigger at the second I want. It starts happening here, now, before my conscious mind knows the danger.

The woman stumbles over an uneven patch of carpeting.

The tray flies. Liquid launches into the air. A goddamn gun won't help me now. A strangled shout of surprised pain. Hot tea spreads across Samantha's white T-shirt, staining it to a pale beige. The woman drops her tote bag filled with books and papers.

"I'm so sorry," the woman says in English. She does sound horrified. Her hands fly to the napkins, grasping, grasping. "Let me help you."

I take her forearm in my fist. "Don't touch her."

My mind works through calculations. Did she come into this car with ill intent? Did she spill the tea on purpose? I'm worried about the hot liquid against Samantha's tender skin, but not so much that I'll loosen my hold on this intruder before I'm sure she poses no danger.

A man appears behind her, one wearing a sharp suit. The same one I saw in the dining car a moment ago. My brother. "I'll question her."

I give my thanks in a nod, nudging her into his custody. Josh and I have our disagreements, but I know I can trust him to interrogate her. Her name. Her purpose. Her deepest fears. He can ferret it out of people without a single overt threat. That leaves me free to drag Samantha forward to the lavatory. She squeaks in either alarm or pain as I close the door, imprisoning us both inside.

My hands are trembling as I pull her T-shirt over her head. So much for a soldier's calm. So much for a goddamn smooth trigger finger. Her skin is red, but the burn doesn't look severe. Thank fuck for the lukewarm water and weak tea. It's soaked her bra, a simple white lace, and I reach around to unhook it. Then she's standing there naked, a half-foot away from me, her nipples hard, her skin pebbling beneath the cool air and my searing gaze. I smooth my palm over her skin, reassuring myself that she's fine, that she's safe, that she's warm in my embrace.

SAMANTHA

I'M NAKED.

Half-naked, technically. I'm still wearing my jeans. Definitely more naked than I ever thought to be in a public restroom. The mirror shows my shoulders, my breasts, my stomach. The view stops there, to make way for a small sink. The sting of the warm tea is long forgotten, erased by the feel of cool air and a hot touch.

Liam dampens a handful of napkins and runs it over my skin. I suck in a breath at the feel of coarse paper over my skin, the brush of his fingertips across my nipples. He doesn't even seem to notice my nudity. His expression is that of a soldier during battle, severe and intimidating.

"Are you hurt?" His voice comes out gravelly.

"No," I say, feeling breathless. "Not really." It did hurt at the time. Or maybe it just shocked me. Finding myself half-naked and in a tiny enclosed space shocked me more than that. There isn't enough room for both of us. There isn't enough oxygen either. The lack makes me breathe more deeply. My breasts move almost enough to brush his shirt.

He dampens another napkin and brushes my skin. "We'll tell the train there's a medical emergency. At the very least you'll need painkillers."

"Please. No. It really doesn't hurt that bad. It mostly took me by surprise."

"Are you sure?" he asks, his green eyes piercing.

A flush rises to my skin that has nothing to do with the hot liquid or the cool napkins. Shivers wrack my body. He said he wouldn't touch me until I played the violin. "You're touching me, you know."

"Only to make sure you're okay." He reaches down to the hem of his own T-shirt, a worn green henley. I can only stare as he yanks it over his head. With no ceremony or warning he pulls it over my head. Then I'm draped in fabric much too large for me, my nipples pressing against the thin cloth. It's almost worse than being exposed, feeling the warm fabric, being surrounded by the masculine scent of him. Now he's the one half-naked.

He turns gruff. "That should keep you warm."

Broad shoulders rest atop a muscled chest. Abs stack down to the waist of his jeans. A dusting of gold-tinted hair covers his skin, lighter than what's on his head. It isn't the first time I've seen him naked. Only a few days ago I poured rubbing alcohol over his wound, but it's not the same when I'm tending to him. Not the same when he's tending to me. We can treat each other's wounds with pure determination. Even now my gaze goes to the white bandage, still in place despite the flurry of action.

"What about you?" I ask, worried now. "Did you hurt—"

He makes an exasperated sound. "I'm fine."

From a deep, unseen spring, amusement bubbles up. "We make a fine pair, don't we? Both of us hurting, both of us pretending it doesn't hurt."

Humor forms emerald lights. Then he sobers. His fingers brush my cheek. "This may not be the time or the place, but I do love you, Samantha Brooks."

A gasp sounds far away. It comes from me. A poignant ache fills me, much more painful than any spill could be. It feels like hope. Words, words, words. I've never been good with them. If I could play him a song with my bow and violin it would be answer enough. Instead I use my fingers a different way. I run them up his biceps, playing an opening chord. And then across his pecs.

His lids dip lower. "What are you doing?"

"This isn't the time or the place," I whisper, leaning forward to kiss his chest. The springy hair tickles my nose. His masculine scent begins a heavy beat in my center.

"It's not," he agrees, but he doesn't stop me. He doesn't leave. Instead he dips his head. His lips nudge mine. I open in explicit invitation. He sweeps his tongue inside, tasting me. "Tea," he mutters. "You taste like tea. You'll never be able to sleep tonight if you have more."

My lips curve beneath his onslaught. "One more cup."

With reluctance he sets me away from him. He opens the door and pulls me after him. There's no sign of the woman or the spilled cup of tea. Josh lounges in one of the empty seats across the aisle. My surprise at seeing him earlier rears again. "You're in France?"

"Apparently," he says with his casual insouci-ance.

Liam reaches overhead to dig through the luggage. I work hard to ignore the way it makes his back muscles flex. He pulls out a shirt and puts it on. "What did you find out?"

A shrug from Josh. "Her name and address."

That makes Liam glare. "Did she lie to you?"

"I saw her passport. It looks legit."

"It was probably just an accident," I say, mostly because I don't want Liam to worry. Also because I don't want to worry, myself. We've only come out of hiding for a few hours. They can't have found me that quickly, can they? Nerves churn in my stomach.

Liam doesn't look convinced. "You said her passport was real?"

"I said it looked legit. Actually, I think it was a fake. A very good one. I already put a tail on her, so we'll see what we find out. Welcome back to the land of living, where there are a disturbing number of people who want you dead."

LIAM

I GAVE SAMANTHA hell for putting down her violin, even for a few months. I berated her for it, resented her, but I can't deny it was effective. Hiding kept her safe. Safe even though I was weakened. Safe enough that it tempted me to stay there forever. Only minutes into Paris there are a thousand eyes upon us. There's a target on her back. Perhaps not this very second, in a crowded train station. Soon. The soldier's instincts tell me that much. It will only take two well-placed bullets to accomplish their tasks. One to take me down, the second for her. They can only touch her over my dead body, but the lingering ache in my side proves that it's possible.

Samantha and I exit the train without my brother, leaving him without a word like the strangers we were when we stepped on board. A mercenary who's done work for North Security meets us with a black SUV. A car leads the way and follows behind.

I lift my wrist to do a security check. "Report. Webb."

"Clear."

"Rogers."

"Clear."

"North."

"Clear," Josh says. I pretend not to notice the sarcasm in his voice. He thinks this is overkill. There are six more checks. All clear. Yes, there are diplomats who don't have such protection. We may have given up anonymity, but at least now I can deploy my full resources. There has to be some compensation.

The place we're going isn't my safe house. Not specifically, but it's as safe as any place we've ever fortified. Frans has been a friend for years. His two-hundred-year-old chateau is outfitted with the latest technology, thanks to North Security. I contacted him when we first crossed from Germany. We could have stayed in the servants' quarters, the grounds large enough that he wouldn't even know we were there, but he extended a formal invitation instead.

He greets us in the foyer with a young woman I've never met. "Fransisco," I say, clasping his hand. "I heard congratulations were in order, but I didn't believe it."

A slight smile. "Thank you. My bride, Isabella Marie Castille."

Mischievous lights twinkle in her dark eyes. Despite her very Spanish name, her manner and accent marks her as American. "Nice to meet you, Mr. North. Fransisco has told me nothing about you. I think he likes to be mysterious."

It's hard to reconcile the playfulness of this Isabella with the strict formality of Frans. He comes from an old aristocratic family. His ancestor was exiled from Spain due to a gentleman's disagreement over a lady a hundred years ago. The title passed to Frans's grandfather during the Spanish civil war. He refuses to take residence in the family property in Catalonia for reasons he's never shared with me. Instead he maintains this home in France, a little bit of irony that a nobleman has found refuge in the land that once beheaded everyone with a title.

"You must be Samantha Brooks," Frans says, bowing over her hand.

Samantha doesn't quite swoon, but it's close. I think it's the suit. Who wears a suit on a Saturday morning? I wear them during certain assignments and formal meetings with our clients, out of necessity more than preference. It's a uniform—the same way fatigues would be during a battle.

Is that a blush staining her cheeks? On the drive she seemed exhausted from the travel. Her eyes are still a little glassy, proving she needs rest more than anything. "Thank you for having us in your home," she says, sounding a little shy. "It's beautiful."

More beautiful than the cold, utilitarian compound I keep in the Texas Hill Country.

Hell, she's turning me into an ass. I'm not the

kind of bastard to get jealous because someone pays her attention. It's always been like this, her presence turning me into someone else. And it's getting worse. I have the urge to brush the pink from her cheeks, to shield her from Frans's eyes, despite the fact that he clearly has a pretty young bride. I want to hide her away, as if we're wolves, as if I can drag her by her nape into a cave where only I get to see her, smell her, taste her.

Isabella drops a curtsey that seems to mock the politeness more than respect it. Her smile implies we're in on the joke with her. "You must be tired from the trip. Call me Isa." She glances at me. "Let me show Samantha her rooms."

Samantha starts to follow her, and I put my hand on her arm. "I'll come with you."

"Do you think I'm going to spirit her away?" Isabella asks with fake severity.

Samantha looks back at me, her beautiful brown eyes soft. She's asking me to let her go, and I realize she wants to be alone with Isabella. Because she hasn't had anyone but me for company for two months. And I've been a surly bastard. The realization makes my chest squeeze. Of course she wants to spend time with someone her own age. *Someone who doesn't blame her for giving up the violin for a short while.* She only did it for me, but that made it worse.

It takes effort to remove my hand and give a curt nod. Permission.

The two women practically skip off, looking so young and innocent that my throat clenches. What the hell am I doing with her? I'm dragging her around the world to slake my lust.

"I know," Frans says, his voice dry. "I must appear the same way when I look at Isa walking away. Like I've been hit over the head with something very heavy."

"Marriage?" I ask, cocking an eyebrow. I'm not the only one slaking my lust.

"It was time. Responsibilities to the title."

"You don't give a fuck about your responsibility to the title."

"Oh yes," he says blandly. "You're right. I'd forgotten about that. How about you and I drink a glass of port while the women talk about us? You can tell me how you almost died and I can tell you how I got married, and we can compare battle scars."

CHAPTER FOUR

Rich classical music phrases, lasting 10 seconds long, cause the heart rate and other parts of the cardiovascular system to synchronize with the music.

SAMANTHA

ISA SHOWS ME to a large set of rooms that looks like it belongs in a period drama. There's plush oriental rugs and gilt furniture. I don't have a single bedroom, the way I expected. Instead there's an actual apartment—a sitting room, a dressing room, and a large bedroom. Velvet drapes surround the bed, revealing a white lace counterpane.

"This is too much," I tell her, twirling in a circle. It makes me feel like a princess.

"I told Frans you might be more comfortable in a smaller room." Her smile turns sly. "He thought you'd want to be near Liam, though. His apartments are through there."

A door stands open, revealing a similar sitting room with more masculine tones. "Oh, I mean probably. For safety reasons. We aren't together."

Even as I say the words the memory of his bare chest in the train restroom flashes across my consciousness. I can see the ripple of strength, scent the musk of salt and man. We aren't together, but we really aren't apart either.

Isa makes a disappointed face. "He's so handsome."

I have to laugh. "Probably a happy new bride thinks everyone should be in love."

"Ohhh." She wanders away, turning back to glance at me over my shoulder. "It wasn't a love match."

That makes me blink. I can only stare at her. Not a love match? What other kind of match is there? She seems to be referencing something like an arranged marriage, but it's the twenty-first century. People don't do that, do they? Then again, this place is drenched in old-world formality.

"I've shocked you," she says cheerfully. "Don't worry. It was all a big shock for me too."

A woman enters the room, her doe-shaped eyes alert, her satin dress reminiscent of a maid. "The luggage is in the dressing room. Can I help mademoiselle unpack?"

"Later," Isa says, her voice hard.

Dangerous undercurrents ripple through the air, making the hair on my arms rise. The woman nods in a way that's both deferent and dominant before she leaves.

"Sorry about that," Isa murmurs. "I know it seems rude, but you can't trust the servants here. They report everything to Frans. If they insist on spying on me, they'll have to work for it."

Surprise steals my voice. "What is this place?"

A soft laugh. "You'll get used to it. Or maybe you won't. If you and Liam aren't an item, that probably means you're going to be a completely ordinary guest. Like Bethany."

"Bethany's here? What about Romeo?"

"They got here two weeks ago."

That's not long after we left Germany and rented a flat in Madame Tissot's house. The similarity prods at my consciousness, until I'm forced to face the truth: Liam has been planning this. It wasn't a moment spurred on by the emotion of the day—or by the fact that I poured rubbing alcohol on his wound like a crazy person. It was always going to end this way.

"There you are," says a familiar voice.

Warmth suffuses me as I take in the sight of Bethany, wearing her leotard and tights as if it's a regular practice day back in Tanglewood before the tour began. She opens her arms, and I almost trip over myself hugging her. She pulls me into a deep embrace.

"I was worried about you," she murmurs against my cheek.

"I was worried about me too," I say, trying to make it a joke. Then I pull back. "I'm sorry about the tour. It must have been a mess when it couldn't continue."

"Please, honey. I wouldn't have kept going if you were in danger." She gives me a little shrug. "Besides, we were technically on loan from Cirque du Monde. Their lawyers had set things up so that we got paid whether the shows happened or not."

That makes me laugh. "That must have given Talent Development a heart attack."

"None of the old label reps are here. There's someone else designing the show."

Unease moves through me, even though it shouldn't matter. The only reason I agreed to do the show is so that I can draw out whoever's behind this. Then Liam can get back to his regular life.

As for me, I'm not sure what a regular life looks like. My tidy little future filled with violin concerts and international acclaim? That shattered along with the wood on the stage of Carnegie

Hall.

Bullets have a way of doing that.

I force a fake, bright smile. "Who's running the show?"

"Some investor in the theater. It might be okay, though. He seems to be more about the skill than the showiness. He let us come up with a new routine."

An image forms of some old, stodgy man in a vest with balding white hair. Maybe he has a more classical taste. He probably won't want something that would be fit for a pop concert. That actually appeals to me. Something more sedate means I won't be flying around the stage doing stunts. Instead I'll wear regular black concert clothes and play songs that—my stomach clenches. This isn't good.

Even the idea of playing makes me feel sick.

Bethany pulls me close to her side as she starts a soft conversation with Isa, as if she understands that I'm too worried to speak right now. They have the patter of comfort. They must have spent time together in the past two weeks, getting close, being friends. While I was a few hundred miles away, trapped alone in a small room with a man who resents me. No, he resents my choices. Is that the same thing? It's hard for me to tell. A discussion of dresses lulls me to the decadent room.

"I had the costume department send something over," Bethany says. "It will fit in well enough, even if I look eccentric. And the skirt falls away so if I need to perform unexpectedly I can."

Isa appears to take the offer seriously, like maybe there are frequently situations where emergency acrobatics and dance take place. "Will Romeo also be in costume?"

Bethany smiles. "He's got a tux."

"What are we dressing up for?" I ask, shivering a little at the re-entry into the conversation. I've grown accustomed to my prison. I find myself missing those walks along the sea. I miss his shadow following me—stalking me and keeping me safe. "I basically just brought jeans."

"It's a ball," Isa explains. "I have a few we can alter for you."

I make a face. Isa has a small frame with voluptuous features. I can only imagine how beanpole thin I'll look trying to wear something made for her. "Maybe we can find something at the mall."

For the first time Isa looks hesitant. Not exactly unsure, but maybe a little embarrassed. "Formal wear would usually work, but since it's

Frans, that means actual ballgowns. I don't want you to feel out of place in a regular dress. Especially since you're the guest of honor."

"The guest of honor?"

"Oh." She looks dismayed. "Liam didn't tell you?"

Unfortunately there's a lot Liam doesn't tell me. "I just don't want to put you through any trouble."

"It's no trouble," Isa says in a confiding tone. "Besides, it will give the maid something to do besides spy on me. Now what do you think looks better on her, Bethany, a royal blue or red?"

Soulful brown eyes examine me. "What kind of red?"

"I'd prefer the blue," I say quickly, mostly because it sounds a little more sedate. I don't necessarily like being at the center of attention, even if the violin often makes it so.

"Bright red," Isa says as if I didn't speak.

"I propose we do something a little fun. Let's use the ballgown but also make it a costume. I have this idea in my head, and I can't shake it. She will stand out so well."

A blush warms my cheeks. "Umm… I don't want to stand out."

Isa smiles. "Your soldier would like it very

much. Actually, he would probably hate it. All the men admiring you in such a bold color. We could make him jealous."

That has a strange appeal—proving to him that I'm admired by more than him. I know that he wants me, even that he loves me, but he can't shake the old sense of control. Another man wouldn't seek to possess me. That's not how modern relationships work.

Then again, this is hardly the place to explain a modern relationship.

"This is a rebirth," Bethany says in her casual wisdom. "Both of the tour and of you. It shouldn't be a soft sound on the world's stage. When this night is over, everyone will know that you're alive."

That's what I'm afraid of. And it's what needs to happen.

LIAM

FRANS LEADS ME through a series of broad hallways until we turn toward his library. A low rumbling warns me from entering. An Irish Wolfhound bares his teeth as I turn the corner. Wiry gray hair rises on the back of his neck. Standing at four feet tall, he would be intimidating to anyone, which explains why the Irish once had an army of three hundred hounds. This particular one lets out a whine when he gets a good sniff. Then I'm attacked by ninety pounds of wriggling happiness, two large paws almost reaching my shoulders. Wolf manages a long lick across my cheek before I playfully push him off. "Down, Wolf."

Wolf doesn't obey. Instead he hops playfully from armchair to armchair, shoving the heavy furniture across the hardwood floors with a screech.

I raise my eyebrows at Frans, who shrugs. "The training didn't stick."

Irish Wolfhounds have been gifts to royalty as far back as the ancient royal times. Wolf was my gift to Frans three years ago, when he was a puppy. He could do *sit*, *stay*, and *down* when I left him. Now he acts more like the puppy he was back then. No discipline. Ironic, considering some of the hobbies Frans entertains. Which reminds me of his recent nuptials.

"Are you going to tell me the real story?" I ask, settling into a chair by the blazing fire. The chill from the train ride seeped into my bones. I still can't shake the memory of that woman's encounter.

"Of my marriage? Once I've had more to drink." Frans begins us down this path by pouring two glasses of brandy. He hands one to me before taking a seat. "That is a story I will share with very few men, but you'll be one of them."

"Dangerous?" I ask, because I'm responsible for security here.

"Not unduly. Scandalous certainly."

That makes me smile. He knows he can share the story with me because my discretion would not allow sharing scandals. For one thing, I'm under an ironclad nondisclosure with North Security. For another thing, I don't give a fuck about scandals. I know some of the people who run in Frans's social circles. International businessmen and displaced royalty. They need services such as mine. They are clients, not friends. Only Frans has crossed that particular line.

"Then I'll wait patiently."

"You may wait patiently, but I have questions that will come sooner than that. Especially since I'm hosting a ball on behalf of the young and beautiful Miss Samantha Brooks."

I manage not to react to the word *beautiful*. "She's off-limits."

An amused look. "I thought I noticed you

acting like a wild animal downstairs. Such base instincts, my friend. I never would have thought you'd feel that way about a woman."

"She isn't an ordinary woman."

"Not ordinary. What sort of people are after her? I read about the events in New York City with concern. I never would have thought you'd get shot, either. Especially in front of a crowd."

"Happy to provide entertainment," I say, taking a sip of the scotch. It goes down smooth. Only the best for the duke. I've learned to navigate this world, but that doesn't mean I want it.

Frans's dark eyes acknowledge my discomfort. He reaches a hand over the armrest to stroke Wolf's head. The dog's eyes roll back in ecstasy. "You never liked expensive spirits."

"Or expensive houses. Expensive clothes."

"That's what you get for charging so much for your services."

A low laugh. "You can afford it."

"And look what I've purchased, a pretty young wife."

"Pardon?" I ask, my tone bland.

"Don't act like you're going to kick my Spanish ass. It wasn't as if I bought her at auction. This is how the old marriages are made. And I like old things. She was willing enough."

Old memories turn my stomach. "Willing enough."

"She agreed to the deal being made to save her family. Her sisters are currently traveling in Italy. Her brother was accepted at Harvard. Her family bears the fruit of her labor."

"Labor that she understood from the start?" Frans has specific tastes that include things most brides wouldn't expect. In other words, he's kinky as fuck. It goes beyond silk blindfolds and padded handcuffs. I don't judge his preferences, but it makes me uncomfortable to think of them visited on the vibrant young woman I met earlier. Especially if she hadn't known in advance.

"It would have been indelicate to go into details during early courting rituals. I make sure she experiences pleasure, if that's what you're concerned about."

"You know it's not." A woman can enjoy what's done to her even if she doesn't want it. The woman I met a few minutes ago hardly looked under duress, but a woman can also hide that part of her from the world. I learned that a long time ago.

"Then don't look so dark and forbidding, my good friend. I don't judge your lust for a woman who was once under your care. For all the pageantry of wealth, men are really just animals. We take what we want. We fuck who we want. We enjoy what we've had the strength to take."

He lifts his glass for a toast, and though I'd like to disagree, it would be hypocritical. Samantha is the only thing I've ever wanted, and I've kept her to me ruthlessly.

The clink of our glass resounds above the quiet crackle of the fire.

"She isn't your mother," he says, so soft I'm almost not sure I heard him.

My heart slams in a heavy beat of anger. Damn him for mentioning it. Damn myself for saying it in a moment of indiscretion, when the smooth slide of the scotch loosened my tongue. "You have no idea what you're talking about."

"I know more than you think. You're not the only person who knows how to investigate someone. Do you think I would let just anyone guard the chateau? You have the keys to the kingdom. Who better to betray me than the one I trusted to protect me?"

Something about his words stick in my memory. The keys to the kingdom. Was that what Samantha's father had? Was that what he transcribed onto her memory? Surely that's the only thing that would be so important, but we don't know what keys or what kingdom.

It wouldn't do to blame Frans for his investigations. Smart, that's what I'd call it. Like he said, I hold the keys to his safety. My natural privacy doesn't adhere to logic. I learned that solitude meant safety too long ago to forget the lesson now. "So you know the history. Don't presume to know my mind."

Eyes almost black as ivory. He stares at me, undaunted. "How much was she sold for?"

Fury flares in my blood, burning hot and red. "You don't want to walk this path."

"Even men who aren't blessed with the pageantry of wealth find a way to be absolutely fucking horrible, don't they? Your father certainly had very little money. She couldn't have cost much."

Scarlet stains my vision. I launch myself at him, slamming my fist into his jaw. Even in my fury I manage to turn the hit so that his body can absorb the blow. Even in my fury, I don't want to kill him. Another punch, this one lands against the side of his eye. That will turn black. I may not want him dead, but I do want him to be hurt. I'm straddling him on the expensive carpet, the fire raging beside us, the dog alternating whines and howls, unable to decide where his loyalties lie.

My fist pulls back to land a final blow before I even see the way Frans reacts to me—he defends himself, the way a body will naturally avoid a fire, but he doesn't hit me back. He wanted me to hit him. Why? I straighten enough to glare at him. "What the fuck? Are you so fucking guilty about buying your bride that you need me to beat the punishment into you?"

A careless laugh as he rubs his jaw. "You didn't mind too much."

I roll onto the carpet, looking up at paintings on the goddamn ceiling. That's how you know you're truly rich, I suppose, when there isn't enough room on the walls for priceless art. It must be embedded into the house. Wolf launches himself between us, rolling over on his back, deliriously happy that our fight ended. I reach over to rub his belly, all the anger drained out in those punches.

"You're a bastard," I say without heat.

"Never more than with her."

Hell. "Should I take her away from here?"

"I would kill you if you tried."

I don't doubt that he would make the attempt. Probably I would live anyway. Despite the bullet that I took in front of a theater full of people, I'm damnably hard to kill. If I weren't my father would have done the deed years ago. Days at a time in disease-ridden water would have killed anyone without an iron will. Pure stubbornness kept me alive. That, and my mother, for as long as she stayed.

CHAPTER FIVE

As a result of the mathematical nature of pitch bracket notation, arithmetic and algebra can be directly applied to the melodies.

SAMANTHA

THE BED IS high enough that I have to hitch myself up as I climb in. Heavy blankets ward away the chill. I close the velvet curtains only halfway though. I want to see the door. Maybe I feel less safe being away from Liam. His apartments may be next door but I haven't seen him since I was shown upstairs. For all I know he could be downstairs with Fransisco.

Or he could have gone into Paris for the evening.

A shadow appears in the doorway.

I know it's him even before my mind can place his silhouette. He brings with him a sense of safety that I've never known anywhere else. And anticipation that feels dangerous. The dichotomy pulls at my insides, ripping them to shreds by the time he crosses the room.

Then he stands at the bed, framed by the velvet curtains.

"You couldn't sleep," he says, his voice quiet. He doesn't need to see me move to know that I'm awake. We've always had that awareness of each other, even when we shouldn't.

"This place is unreal."

He laughs softly. "A far cry from North Security headquarters?"

"A far cry from anywhere." Shyness tightens my throat, but I've lived for too long in the shadow of my past. "I'd like it if you held me. For comfort." And for more, although I'm not bold enough to spell it out.

He hesitates long enough I think he's going to refuse.

Then he sits on the bed beside me. He lies down on top of the covers, still wearing his clothes. He even has his boots on. Hardly the intimacy I was hoping for, but when he pulls me close, I sigh in repletion. A kiss to my crown that doesn't end. His breath stirs my hair.

The warmth soothes me the way I hoped, but I can't shake the feeling that we're not alone in this bed, that old ghosts followed him into the room, that they hover around us now, dark and insistent. "This place is like a freaking castle," I whisper, and his lips curve in a smile. "And my father actually liked to stay at nice places when we traveled before."

"It took some getting used to after the barracks in the army."

He has talked about his time in the army, even though I know there's a lot that's classified. That part I understand. It's what comes before that's still a mystery. He told me about the well. About how his father would throw him down there. It's very little to know about someone's childhood. Enough to make me afraid to learn more. Is it possible to know the man without his past? Can anyone appear fully formed without being impacted every day from what came before?

"And your house before the army," I say, bracing myself, fortifying my courage against what I'm sure will be a brick wall. Possibly I'll even face his scorn. He won't like this.

He stiffens, but he doesn't immediately push me away. That's better than I expected. The ghosts around us seem to stir, as if some of them came from the past. As if they like being mentioned.

"Yes," he says, his voice low. "Different from that."

It's not much of an invitation, but more than he's ever shown before. I feel like someone navigating an ancient temple filled with traps. One wrong step, and I might be faced with flying arrows or boulders with spikes running down a ramp. "What was it like instead?"

A long silence. The ghosts become thick in the room.

"It was… dirty. That's the main thing I remember. There was barely enough money for food. Definitely none for Windex. Even the water came out brown from the tap, as if nothing there could ever be pure."

My heart squeezes. "I'm sorry."

"I think living in the woods would have been cleaner, actually. At least there would have been fresh air. We lived in such filth that the bugs had a field day. They feasted on us, until it felt more like their home than ours."

A heave of my stomach. "You don't have to—"

"Disgusting, isn't it? I learned to pick fleas and ticks off my body the way other children fiddle with the controls of a video game. I never expected to be free of them completely. They stuck to my skin. They climbed into my eyes while I slept because they liked the moisture."

I sit up abruptly with a useless wave of my

hand, as if I can bat the ghosts away. Of course they aren't real. They're inside him. Inside Liam. "I wish I could meet your father," I cry, tears in my eyes. The moisture that fleas would seek. "I would hit him over and over again. I would hurt him."

A soft chuckle. "So bloodthirsty. Perhaps you and I aren't so different after all."

"Wasn't there someone? A teacher or—"

"My mother did her best while she was there. She would wash our clothes in the powdered soap we purchased in bulk. It dried outside in the sun, where the heat could kill anything living there. At least until it was brought back inside the house. It was worse when she left. Most of the teachers knew better than to confront my father. They might find someone waiting for them at night."

His mother left. My mother left. It leaves a hole of a certain shape that can never be filled. It's always there, wondering why you weren't good enough. I put my hand over his chest, feeling the way the breath rises and falls. "Why did she go?"

"Why did she stay as long as she did? That's the question. I suppose I'm the reason."

Tears burn behind my eyes. "You blame yourself."

"After Elijah I suppose she realized it would

never end. It was a rough delivery. There was no doctor. She must have known my father would continue getting her pregnant until she finally died."

"Have you looked for her?" It's something North Security does—find people. They trade in information even more than weapons. That's the world we live in.

"No." A wealth of emotion hides beneath the steel of his voice. "Why should I?"

"Because she's your mother." If mine hadn't died I would have sought her out. Of course, if mine hadn't died I would have gone to her when my father was thought dead.

I never would have met Liam North.

"Not anymore."

Sympathy rises like a fine mist. "You're angry at her. I understand that but—"

"I'm not angry at her. I'm angry at myself. What would I say to her? I'm sorry that I let him rape you in the room next to mine. I'm sorry that I covered my ears instead of listen to you beg him." He flips me over in a rough flash, and I'm facing the bed, a weight behind me. His breath warms my temple. "I'm sorry he hurt you for so long because you wanted to make sure I was fed."

Tears dampen the sheets beneath my cheek.

"Liam."

"It wouldn't be a sweet reunion, Samantha."

"You're hurting me," I say, even though it isn't exactly true. It doesn't hurt, the way my arms are held down. *You're scaring me.* That's what I really mean. He lifts some of the weight on my back, but he doesn't let me go. I'm his prisoner. It's like I've awakened a beast inside him, one who won't be satisfied until he tastes first blood.

LIAM

FEAR. PAIN. GRIEF. The scars from a lifetime ago burn across my skin.

A heavy heartbeat pounds in my chest. It's like I'm in battle, but I'm not fighting the slim form beneath me. I'm fighting a formless enemy—the past. Samantha should know what she's tempting with these questions.

I would hit him over and over again. I would hurt him.

Of course she would. Justice makes sense to her. She loves me with the wholehearted purity that a ward can love a guardian. I saved her from a life of drudgery in that orphanage. And probably death, from whoever hunts her now. Only a fool would assume gratitude has nothing to do with it.

My knee presses between her legs. She stiffens as she senses my intent.

"What are you doing?" she whispers, her voice muffled against the mattress.

Does she sound afraid? I'm depraved enough to prefer it. "You said you wanted me to hold you. For comfort. That's what I'm doing, little prodigy."

"This isn't comfortable."

I press my face to her neck, breathing in deep. It's a fully animal bondage, scenting her where she's the most vulnerable, brushing my nose against her nape so she shivers. "It isn't?" I press a kiss to the top of her spine. "I'll have to try harder."

My other knee pushes her legs farther apart. In this position I can press my erection to her core. I don't plan to fuck her right now. I'm not quite sane enough for that. There's the chance I could hurt her, and there is no pleasure in the world that would make me risk it. I can rut against her, though. Again and again until she moans low and reluctant, her little hands forming fists in the bedcovers.

"Wait," she gasps out. "Wait. Wait."

Red tints my vision. I'm not the man who's taken care of her all these years. I'm not the man who waits because she's nervous about the pressure on her clit. "I'm sorry if that wasn't the foreplay you wanted, hearing about my mother getting raped. It was a better outcome than some of the women who came on that truck. She was sold to a man who married her. Most men won't do that."

Her body stills beneath me. "What truck?"

"Didn't I mention? My mother was imported from Mexico. Like avocados. Or little sombrero hats that hang on rearview mirrors. She cost a few hundred dollars. And she was young enough that most men who wanted a girl would keep her in a basement somewhere. My father was the kind of bastard who didn't care that other people knew he bought her young."

Shivers wrack her body, and I realize she's crying.

Disgust turns my stomach. I force myself to back away from her. I'm kneeling on the bed, touching her in zero places, and still I can feel the imprint of her body. "Now you know what I am. The devil inside me? It doesn't care about how old you are or whether you want this."

She looks over her shoulder, tear tracks glistening on her cheeks. My heart stops at the picture of her despair. What have I done to her?

"How dare you," she says, her voice low. "You aren't him. You aren't anything like him."

"Haven't you heard me—"

"Oh, I've heard you. I've heard that you think you're using me. And you're just waiting for me to leave, aren't you? That's why you refuse to open up to me, because you think that one day I'm going to disappear like your mother did."

I stare at her helplessly, unsure why she doesn't see the truth of the statement. She's the one kneeling, but she has all the power right now. I'm a supplicant behind her.

She stretches her body far enough that her pretty little ass touches my groin. I suck in a breath. "Samantha. You shouldn't do that. I don't have any control."

"That's right." Her voice comes out caustic. "There's a devil inside."

"Don't tempt me, little prodigy. I want to prove how much it's true."

"I'm not afraid of you." Another press of her ass. She's turned into a little cock tease. "Show me what's so scary. Show me how you're going to act like your father."

It's wrong to touch her with the memory of my father on her lips. With the tragedy of my mother on her mind. I should definitely walk away. Find a bottle of vodka. Lose myself in a hard, dreamless sleep. Instead I nudge my cock against her sex. "Like this."

"By making me feel good?" Her tone challenges me to do worse.

I reach around her body and slip my hand beneath her panties. Smooth skin. Warm damp. I find her clit with unerring precision. There's no slow unfolding. My touch forces her towards an orgasm. Her shattered breath reveals how close she is. A pinch between my thumb and forefinger. That's all it takes for her to buck against me in a wild climax. It's both punishment and reward for standing up to me. I cup her pussy in wordless possession as she comes back into her body.

Another nudge with her ass. I flinch from the pleasure.

"What about you?" she whispers.

"There's no comfort for me," I murmur, pressing a kiss to her temple. I settle her carefully on the bed, exactly like I found her, except her limbs are more lax. Part of her wants to object, but the endorphins have their way. They drag her down into dreams, leaving me to hold her through the night.

CHAPTER SIX

The piano has over 12,000 parts, 10,000 of which are moving.

JOSH

IT PROBABLY LOOKS like I'm lost to the world, fists flying against the bag, sweat dripping down my body, a long stretch of violence tainting the air. She probably thinks I don't notice her. I can't look directly. That would scare her away, like a hare running to ground. There's only the impression of her in the mirror—her long body encased in a leotard and tights, her dark hair pulled high.

Apparently Bethany uses the gym for her own practice.

That means I'm the intruder. Well, thank God for small favors.

Liam prefers to use the outside for his practice. A ten-mile run interspersed with push-ups and other old-fashioned drills. He'd probably climb a fucking tree like Tarzan. I prefer the air-conditioned sterility of a high-end gym, such as the one in the duke's chateau.

I planned to find her, but this is better. There's more than enough room for both of us to practice here. A large area with mats and mirrors. Training equipment. A sauna. There's even a goddamn hot tub for soothing aching muscles, and I spare a thought to imagining Bethany using it naked, the way the bubbling water would obscure and reveal her.

Is she brave enough to come inside when I'm here? If she runs away I'd follow her.

One, two. One, two. Even knowing she's there doesn't blunt my blows to the bag. Hell, it probably makes them more powerful. The sexual frustration has to go somewhere. I feel her eyes on me. It occurs to me that she's doing more than hiding right now. More than deciding whether or not to come in. She's watching me. Maybe admiring me? Lusting after me? *Fuck.*

Even the possibility makes me hard.

I tossed my shirt down an hour ago. My muscles are bunched and thick from hard use. She works with athletic men in her fancy Cirque du Monde, but there's a difference between muscles made for performance and those honed on the battlefield.

Sweatpants hang low on my hips. Low

enough I can imagine pushing them down with Bethany on her knees in front of me. It wouldn't matter that I'm sweaty. She'd hold her mouth open, her tongue pink and pointed. I'd pump my dick until I spilled white come across her lips.

With the image in my mind I have to stop punching the bag. I rest my forehead against the leather, panting, fighting the urge to touch her.

What a terrible fucking time she chooses to finally enter.

"Hello, Josh," she says in such a reasonable, calm tone that I'm desperate to press her against the mirror. I want to smear it with her spit, her sweat. Her come. It takes a decent amount of effort to calm the boil in my blood. I'm still erect when I turn around. No hiding that in fucking sweatpants.

"You decided to come in?"

She notices, of course. Her brown eyes widen. God, if she didn't look so much like a doe caught in the woods. "I knew you wouldn't bother me in Fransisco's house."

"You knew that, did you?"

She turns away dropping a bottle of water against the wall. "Don't stop on my account. I'm going to use the treadmill to warm up before I use the mats."

Here's the thing. She has to bend over to put her water bottle down, which means revealing her ass in its tight glory. If it were a little less perfect, maybe I could have walked away. I could have turned around and punched the bag hard enough to break my hand—and maybe that would kill my boner.

Probably not, though.

"Don't you stretch first?" I ask, grabbing a towel from a bench. I wipe my face, doing my best to appear harmless. It's a bit like a wolf putting on a granny cap and climbing into bed.

"Yes." She draws out the word, stalling.

Of course she stretches first. You're *supposed* to stretch first, and Bethany is a rule follower. Which makes me want to create rules for her to follow. "I'll help you."

It's a completely normal offer between workout partners. We aren't exactly partners, but the private facility creates a sort of intimacy. Her expression wavers. "I'm not sure."

"What are you worried about? You already said I won't bother you in Fransisco's house."

She's smart enough to recognize the threat inherent in my words. And polite enough to still consider letting me touch her lithe body. I would bend her legs far apart, giving her the perfect stretch. Only when she was completely warm would I consider touching her inappropriately.

"It's probably not a good idea," she says, taking a step back. It doesn't appear to be conscious, that step. It's the natural move away from danger. Walking away from a ledge. "You and I don't exactly get along. I promise not to disturb your workout, though."

"It's a little late for that promise," I say with a wry laugh, glancing down at my erection. Hope springs eternal, even though she's unlikely to give it up in the next few minutes.

A blush darkens her cheeks. Her chest rises and falls a little quicker. Well, well. She's not immune to me. Then again, I already knew that. It wouldn't be so fun to tease her if she didn't mind.

"I'm not going to apologize," she says. "I haven't done anything wrong."

"Wrong," I say, tasting the words. "Is it wrong to have a tight little body? Wrong to make me lust after you? Wrong to make me imagine that pretty little mouth wrapped around my—"

"You're trying to scare me, but it won't work."

"I'm not trying to scare you. I'm trying to turn you on." Her eyes have dilated. Nipples press against the stretchy material of her leotard. Oh yes, it's working.

"God, don't you have someone else to bother."

I turn around, because looking at her only makes the ache harder to bear. A hard punch to the bag reverberates through my body. Fight or flight. "So many, Bethany. You have no fucking idea."

CHAPTER SEVEN

In a study of music in dreams, nearly half of the recalled music was non-standard, suggesting that original music can be created in dreams.

SAMANTHA

A MAID WAKES me up at 7 a.m. on the day of the ball. I'm led to the duchess's apartments, which make my set of rooms look tiny.

"I'm used to doing my own before the shows," I say, hoping that I won't have to be fussed over. I'm also hoping that I don't end up trapped in a chair for hours. The ball doesn't start until 8 p.m.

I have a ritual involving black dresses and lip gloss. The tour added liquid eyeliner and some glitter to my cheeks so that my expressions would be more visible from far away. We're still talking about fifteen minutes, not a full day of preparations.

Isa exclaims with a weird amount of excitement for early in the morning and gives me a hug. Bethany appears from behind a swath of red fabric, her hair pulled back in a ponytail. I'm relieved that neither of them look primped, even if Isa's disconcertingly enthusiastic.

"We're going to be bugs," she says.

"Excuse me?" It occurs to me that I might still be asleep. This could be a dream.

Only Bethany looks slightly amused, which lends realism to the experience. "I had this idea when I saw you last night, that you were like a ladybug. They mean good luck."

My gaze falls to a mountain of a red dress. Like a ladybug. It looked pretty but maybe a little disturbing. "I'm not sure how I feel about being a bug."

"Told you so," Isa says to Bethany. "That's why we're going to do it with you. My lady's maid has been sewing since nine o'clock last night. I'm going to be a monarch butterfly. Obviously."

I turn to Bethany. "What are you going to be? A dragonfly?"

"Ooh, that's actually a good idea. I already had a different idea, though. I'm going to be a bumble bee." She gestures to two fashion forms standing in the corner of the room. A ballgown of deep orange is streaked by symmetrical black designs, giving the impression of wings. The yellow gown beside it is broken only by a single thick band of black at the waist. Both of them are gorgeous and classy—the whole insect thing more of a suggestion than actual costume.

"So I just wear a red dress?" I ask hopefully.

"Don't be silly," Isa says, turning the red mountain of fabric upright so it resembles a dress. "We have this black netting that will resemble the spots."

The black netting falls to the sides of the skirts, parting to reveal the red silk in its uncovered sheen in the middle. I have to admit it looks beautiful. Probably more beautiful if I didn't know it was trying to be a bug. I'm not what you'd call an outdoorsy person. Perhaps it is more alluring with the hint of a story behind it. Much like a performance becomes deeper with a sense of character.

The three dresses look striking side by side—red, orange, and yellow. The color of flame. We'll stand out in any gathering of well-dressed people. We'll be the center of attention even before people know our names. Looking at Isa's contentment I know that was the purpose. She leaves to consult with an army of stylists and makeup artists in the large dressing room next door.

"I can't believe you went along with her," I murmur to Bethany.

She laughs softly. "It was my idea. Remember, I'm a performer at heart. How we dress is part of that. How we hold ourselves comes from how we dress."

I look down at her plain tank top. Her black sweat pants are loose fitting and then cinch at her ankles. It's a look that can only look good on someone with an incredible body, which she definitely has. "How are you holding yourself now?"

"This isn't a performance. Think of this room like backstage. In that ballroom downstairs, there will be representatives from the European record label. There will be investors from the theater, including the one who's the creative director of our show. Not to mention half of France's high society, specifically the kind of people who patronize classical music."

Nervousness tightens my throat. Even the idea of playing the violin again makes me seize up. Tonight I won't be playing, but it will be the precursor. The chug-chug-chug to the top of the roller coaster that I don't want to be on. "So I should hold myself with humility in request of their patronage?"

"Oh God no. You should be haughty and intellectual and snobby."

She looks serious. "Snobby?"

"They want to know that there's a secret club to the world of classical music. And that you're part of it. You're their entrance. You're their only hope of being part of it."

"There's no secret club. Or if there is, I'm not part of it."

A musical laugh. "You are the club, Samantha."

"Have you been having conference calls with Liam? He's convinced I'm going to be the star of the show. I mean I expect that kind of optimism from my agent, but you guys know me. I'm just a regular person."

Bethany leads me to a table that's laid out with a large breakfast. "Have a croissant, regular person," she says, piling fresh fruit onto her plate.

I should probably go for fruit or oatmeal or something healthy. The pile of croissants looks flaky and delicious, though. Bethany knows me too well. I grab a croissant and tear a piece to eat. *Yes.* Buttery croissants are the best. My mouth is still full of savory flavor when Bethany holds up her phone. It's my Instagram account. I recognize the photo from the tour. *Violinist. Croissants.*

Eiffel tower. Your favorite child prodigy all grown up. Music emojis complete the bio. The account had been active during the tour, but I assumed it had been abandoned when we left. Apparently not. There are words of affirmation and pictures from around the world, as if I were sightseeing instead of hiding from people trying to kill me. It's the number at the top right that makes my heart stop. My mouth drops open. "One million followers? Who are these people?"

"They're your fans," Bethany says before eating a piece of pineapple.

Somehow I've become a little celebrity. When did this happen? How?

Suddenly the concert at Palais Garnier makes more sense. As does the ball tonight filled with high society and actual royalty. Feeling almost numb with wonder, I click the link in the bio to the tickets being sold for the concert. It's my name headlining the tour. My silhouette holding a violin that's the main image. The concert is already sold out. Resale tickets are going for thousands of euros each.

The career I thought I would have to spend decades building, the one I thought I'd walked away from… it's waiting for me downstairs. It's already mine.

LIAM

I WATCH THE ball from the edges of the room, strolling behind large potted plants and wide columns. A few of the guests are clients of North Security. Most of them are strangers.

"Do you really think they'd make a move here?" Josh asks in the earpiece. I can see him strolling along the ballroom on the opposite side. We have men stationed outside the chateau and throughout the public rooms. We're taking point on the ballroom itself.

"No, but I think they'll attend. Why wouldn't they?" Any chance to survey your opponent was important, especially if your opponent had been in hiding for months.

"That assumes they can get an invitation."

The ball is definitely exclusive, but someone who has the power to destroy a classified file in the US government has high connections. "Tell me about the woman from the train."

There's quiet over the radio. My body tightens. There was something there. Damn it. He clears his throat. "Anthony followed her off the train and lost her on the Avenue du Choisy. We found her ticket information. Her passport was a fake."

"Christ. I should have kept her."

"The French government wouldn't have taken kindly to our holding people hostage on trains," Josh says dryly. "We wanted to come in without too much attention."

"And yet we had someone's attention."

"Someone in Frans's entourage?"

"Maybe. Do we have information on his new wife?"

"You don't trust her?"

"I don't trust anyone."

A low laugh. "He'll kick your ass if he finds out we investigated her. She comes from old money. Railroads, steel, technology. Nothing even remotely connected to politics."

"And now a duchess."

"In other words, she has no incentive to sell out her country."

"Her old country. Now she's a citizen of Spain. A resident of France. And you're forgetting the less frequent reason people sell out their countries. Not always money. It could be ideology."

Josh snorts. "It's always about money."

He might be right about that. Even when people claim they do things for ideological reasons, money usually factors into the equation. Unfortunately we don't know who knew about our location. We can't even be sure that the woman went into our car on purpose. My mind's eye remembers her dark hair and dark eyes, her tanned skin heavily wrinkled. Her clothes were plain—probably too plain. Chosen to be nondescript. Even so, something about her feels familiar.

A stir in the crowd turns their attention to the grand staircase.

A man at the bottom of the stage announces Isa, including her full name and royal titles. She appears at the top of the stairs, wearing a wide gown of orange and black. Despite the rather playful image she projected when I met her, she appears regal now. No one would question her position the way she holds her head, her shoulders, the way she drifts down with regal hauteur, even in whispers.

The man at the bottom announces Bethany. Somehow she manages to make a bright yellow color look mysterious instead of like sunshine. She drifts down the stairs with the grace of a dancer. A murmur of interest spreads across the room as some know that she's part of the concert.

Every muscle in my body tenses. I know who's coming next.

There are strict regulations regarding where I

need to stand to always see the whole crowd. There are protocols for how often I scan the crowd. There are affectations so that people don't notice me or know where my attention goes. All of this is built into my muscles. All of this is thoughtless, but I can't remember it now. Not when every cell in my body leans towards those stairs.

Not when I want to be at her side, escorting her into the room. Marking my possession so that every man who admires her knows exactly where she belongs.

She appears at the top of the stairs. My breath catches. *My God.*

I'm used to seeing her in demure black clothes when she plays. During the tour she wore that costume of blue satin and white lace. It empha-sized her youth. Now she wears a red ballgown that declares her sensuality in dangerous certainty. My cock hardens in the tux with nowhere to go. A rustle goes through the crowd. They know who she is, but that's not the only reason. I can only imagine the ideas running through the men. The gown features a strapless bodice that shows off her small breasts. My fingers twitch at my side. I want to touch her, to tweak her nipples.

A pause. She doesn't immediately come down

the stairs the way the other women did. She stands very still, but I sense her nerves. The crowd must seem intimidating. I never should have let her come in on her own. I take a step forward, determined to walk up the stairs and escort her down.

Her chin lifts.

There's no comparison. She floats down the stairs with such confidence everyone forgets the moment of uncertainty. Everyone except me. Satisfaction suffuses my chest. The part of me that helped raise that young woman feels pride. The rest of me? Pure lust. I want her wearing that dress, the red fabric thrown up around her waist as I pound into her on the marble stairs. I want her bent over, only her pretty little ass visible, framed by the dress, while I sink two fingers into her heat.

"Close your mouth," a low voice mutters directly in my ear. "You have at least two hours before you can drag her away from the ballroom, by the way."

Fucking Josh. Even from across the room he could tell how dumbstruck she makes me. I speak into my mouthpiece. "Noah. Move inside the ballroom. You're taking over the south wall."

The crowd has already swallowed her, greeting

her, taking up her attention. I don't begrudge them her time and space. I don't begrudge them her music. I'm not so possessive that I won't let her perform in whatever capacity, whether it's in the violin or as the belle of the ball, but I want every man who admires her to know she goes home with me at the end of the night.

For that matter, I want no doubt in *her* mind either.

I may not get to keep her, but for right now she's mine.

CHAPTER EIGHT

French composer and virtuoso pianist Louise Farrenc was twice awarded the Prix Chartier of the Academie des Beau-Arts and was appointed to the prestigious position of Professor of Piano at the Paris Conservatory. Despite this, she was paid less than her male counterparts. Only after she composed a piece for the popular and handsome male violinist Joseph Joachim did she finally receive equal pay.

SAMANTHA

MY CHEST TIGHTENS with everybody that brushes against me. There are too many people. I'm reminded of those days in the orphanage, when we were stacked six-deep in a room, the sleeping mats more narrow than our skinny bodies. The irony is that I'm wearing a dress that costs enough to feed the girls there for a year. Faces dance in front of me, a kaleidoscope of bright smiles and shimmery jewels. I want nothing more than to be bundled onto the high bed in my room. Those velvet drapes would shield me from this. I manage to murmur polite greetings without really understanding. *So nice to* *meet you. Oh, thank you. You're so kind.* Hopefully my responses match up to what people are actually saying. It's a buzzing sound, perhaps the language of butterflies and ladybugs and bumble bees.

"Samantha Brooks." A low voice breaks through the crowd. "You look all grown up. And somehow, so much the same. Do you remember me? Probably not."

The person speaking is too handsome to possibly forget except… I search my memory. Nothing. My cheeks feel warm. There's no empty response to this. "I'm so sorry."

He laughs, a little self-deprecating. "I'm sure it's a good thing that I don't look like my teenaged self. Besides the fact that I could barely bring myself to look at you then. Alexander Fox. Above-average cello player. We once played on the same stage in Leningrad."

Surprise disarms me. Probably his handsome face does, too. He could be an actor in a blockbuster movie with those blue eyes and square jaw. "I remember Leningrad."

"I was one of eight cellos in the orchestra. I was so nervous about the performance I was lucky not to fumble my parts. You, however, were a goddamn miracle."

A blush. "Thank you. I'm sorry I don't re-member—"

He waves his hand. "It would be strange if you did. Especially since I know what happened six months after that performance. I could never get you out of my head after that."

Six months after that performance my father died. The servants at the house had no idea where to place me. I ended up at a Russian orphanage. Only later did I find it strange. Shouldn't I have returned to the United States? Unless someone didn't want me there. Unless someone thought it would be easier to kill me in a foreign country, in a house that barely counted all the girls in its care.

Liam North retrieved me from the orphanage and took custody of me. A judge made his guardianship official a few months later. It took money to pull that off. Power. I've always been at the mercy of men. It was only the violin that made it bearable. And now, even that is gone.

Alexander frowns. "I've upset you. Of course I have, bringing that up. I'm a bastard. Let me get you a drink. Distract you. Or would you like to dance?"

I open my mouth, only to find a laugh com-ing out. He sounds a little nervous, but somehow I find it charming. Is this what it would feel like to meet a handsome man at a ball? I suppose that's what I'm doing now, but my past taints every interaction. "You know what? Yes. I would love to dance."

That's how I end up twirling on the parquet floor, the world spinning as if I hang from the ceiling in the Tanglewood theater, everything moving too fast. Instead of a rope and cable around my waist there's a man's warmth.

"I didn't think you'd say yes," Alexander says.

"I didn't think you'd ask me to dance," I say, laughing a little.

"It's been, what? Eight years now? I hope I've learned how to speak to pretty girls better than I could back then. Anything's better than staring at the floor."

"You're a charmer," I say, but I don't seem to mind.

He's lacking the edge of self-destruction that tinged Harry March's interactions. Instead Alexander seems… genuine. He's also handsome. And he knows how to dance. I realize that I didn't really know how when I agreed, but he leads me through the waltz with sure feet.

His blue eyes reflect the light of a thousand crystals on chandeliers. He blows out a breath. "Okay, I'm not that smooth with pretty girls. I should have opened with this, I'm in charge of the concert."

"Oh." I can't control the way my body stiffens. After the harshness of the label reps in the US and the disaster that ended it, I'm sensitive to whoever will call these shots.

"I can only imagine you're nervous about performing again. Rest assured we're working with the best security consultants to make sure that you'll be safe on this stage."

That's what he thinks I'm worried about? It's surprisingly astute. "You've met Bethany, right? She mentioned that you preferred a more classical style."

"I suppose you could say that. I prefer more of a recital format. As far as the dramatic flair... I don't mind it, but I think a little goes a long way. Unless you like a more colorful style? I saw footage of the US tour, but we frequently have license to change things for the European leg."

"A recital style sounds much better to me." That's a lie. Anything where I have to play the violin makes me break out into a sweat. But this way means I'll spend less time onstage.

There will be very little showmanship. Maybe I'll actually manage to survive it...

My stomach cramps. Then again maybe not.

"The truth is…" A lock of hair falls over his forehead, making him look both dashing and shy. "You could probably convince me to do the concert any way you like. You're the headliner for a reason. And I knew your genius when I heard you play eight years ago."

The flattery expands my chest. "Are you performing, too?"

"Oh God, no. My above-average skill as a teenager has fallen to purely mediocre. No, I went to work for an auction house after college. A lot of rubbing elbows and knowing the right people. In the end it was hard to see the best instruments in the world go to billionaires who would lock it up instead of the performers who could make magic."

I murmur my understanding, because so many of the old instruments are owned by museums and investment groups and billionaires. The average musician must save up a lifetime or use a loan. It's not only the upfront cost of the instrument, which can run in the millions, but also the upkeep. I'm one of the rare musicians who owns a masterpiece outright—and that's only thanks to Liam North. He made Lady Tennant, my violin, a gift to me. And I repaid that thanks by locking the violin away. Acid rises in my throat. It's wrong, wrong, wrong, but I can't imagine going back now. I turned my back on more than Lady Tennant that terrible night in New York City, afraid that Liam would die in my arms. I turned my back on music.

"So where do you work now?" I force myself to ask.

Blue eyes study me as if he knows the dark direction of my thoughts. When he speaks I know it's more a kindness than a conversation. "I have another confession to make. My family is one of those overly rich, undertalented people who own some of the best instruments. It's why they pushed me to play the cello. They wanted a prodigy. Instead they got me."

Sympathy tightens my throat. There had been many stage moms and dads when I performed as a child prodigy. They had pointed to me as the example. *You don't want this for them,* I wanted to shout. Better to be normal. Better to be happy. Not that it mattered. They couldn't manufacture prodigy-like skill any more than I could pretend I knew what to do a on playground. "I'm sorry," I say.

"Ah, don't apologize. My father accepted it soon enough. Mom took a little bit longer, but she wants me to be happy. And they're rich enough that they can sponsor prodigies every year.

I took over the family business, managing our investments in the music world. Including with the Palais Garnier."

"It's privately owned?"

"No, but they lease the space to our production company. In other words, we carry the risk if a performance should flop. The Paris Opera gets paid either way."

"Well," I say with a nervous laugh. "We'll try not to flop then."

Of course, that probably means I'll have to play the violin. Yes, that's almost certainly going to be required for any sort of concert. Acid burns my stomach. If only we had stayed in Nantes another week. Another month. Another year. I never wanted to return to the real world.

LIAM

SHE LOOKS LIKE a princess in the center of the ballroom. And the fucker holding her? He looks like a prince. I can't ignore who that makes me in this story. The villain. The one who wants to drag her down to the basement where no one can touch her. Only me.

The veneer of respectability wears thin. I'm bursting with primal impulse, with violent lust. I want to howl at the goddamn moon. Instead I cross the ballroom and tap his shoulder.

"May I cut in?" I ask, with regular words. *Congratulations,* I tell myself, mocking the impulse that brought me here, *you didn't snarl or snap at the other male trying to mate her.*

He looks reluctant, but there's no way for him to politely refuse. That's his first mistake, favoring politeness over this woman. She's worth rudeness. She's worth everything.

Then she's in my arms, and I sweep her away.

Her brown eyes examine me. "You know how to waltz?"

I glance down at my tux, my shined shoes, the neat steps that lead her through the dance. "I know how to do many things that make me fit into places like this."

"Places like a fancy ball? Or places that aren't battlefields?"

Damn her for seeing more than she should. "I told you how I was raised."

"Bullshit."

A hesitation in my step. I don't trip, but it's a close thing. I can count the number of times she's used swear words on one hand, most of them when Josh tried to teach her to swear. "Pardon?"

"I called bullshit. You came from a place infested with fleas, but that's not who you've been for years. For decades. So why do you use that as an excuse?" Dark lashes drop to pale white cheeks. "Unless you think that I'm nothing more than I was. Unless I'm still the girl in that orphanage."

"You were only there for two weeks." The words are out before I can stop them. Too much history. Too much guilt. The ordinary amount of guilt is heavy enough, the weight of wanting to fuck her pretty red lips when I should be protecting her.

Her gaze meets mine. "You never told me why."

"Why I adopted you?"

"Why you waited two weeks to do it."

Hell. The ballroom becomes a minefield. If I take a wrong step, she's the one who blows up. "I wasn't sure what would happen to you. I thought someone else might take custody of you."

She seems to accept that without further question. Relief is a faint vibration. I won't know it fully until the song ends. "And then you realized no one else was coming."

Sadness colors her words. Maybe embarrassment. Better those feelings than if she knew the truth. "I knew I could never be a decent guardian for you, that I could never provide a real family.

You were so young. So strong. I had to try anyway."

"Because you killed my father. And almost killed me."

I glance at the couple dancing near us. Thankfully they haven't heard. It wouldn't be ideal for my rogue actions as a former US agent to be broadcast to French society. Her safety is the primary concern. More than the fact that I want to fuck her.

More than whether or not she likes that young man she danced with before me.

"Tomorrow we'll record the songs he made you memorize." Our hiding was complete enough that she couldn't play the violin. Her skill would have been too remarkable. So would visiting a recording studio. "That will allow us to run them through some algorithms. And it will also be used—"

She appears calm. "In case I die before we solve the mystery?"

"No. I'm not planning for that." Every cell in my body rebels against the idea. The soldier in me understands collateral damages. It understands statistics. The man wants to hold Samantha close. I'll burn down the world before I let it singe her. "It will be used as an insurance policy."

"I already wrote down the sheet music."

I'm distracted by the feel of her slender waist, by the warmth of her small hand on my arm. It's enough that I almost miss the tremor in her voice. "The music may have some nuance the notes miss. We'll be able to run it through some databases once it's digitized."

She doesn't answer, but I feel a stiffness in her body. I want to soothe it in the most primal way, to stroke her, caress her, until she surrenders to safety.

"I thought you'd want to play, anyway. It's been months."

"Not that."

No, she wouldn't have good memories attached to that song. I hate that her original composition started with that melody. As if he taints everything about her, even her inspiration. Even her mind. The composition strays from the notes he gave her, but it doesn't erase the way it starts. I suppose it's like she said. *Unless you think that I'm nothing more than I was.* She is more than a frightened girl under her father's control, but it always starts with that.

She turns her face toward the orchestra, her natural instinct toward the music. In the profile her expression looks haunted. I study her full lips, her upturned nose, struck by a feeling of déjà vu.

"Are you afraid?" That's how she looks—afraid. Of the violins? Of the music?

That earns me a hollow laugh. "Of course not. How can I be afraid with my own private army following me everywhere. You even brought Josh on the train. I thought that poor woman would have a heart attack when he insisted on questioning her."

"The woman." The dancers around me slow down. Maybe it's just my heartbeat.

"She felt bad for spilling the tea."

"It wasn't an accident." My mind has been running the tape of that moment enough times to be certain of that, even before Josh spoke earlier. "Her passport was fake. Did you recognize her?"

Samantha gives me a strange look. "Of course not. I would have said something if I knew who she was. But I did think... she looked familiar. Is that weird?"

Not weird. Too much of a coincidence considering I felt the same thing.

The quartet builds a crescendo. The floor around us clears for a second. I take the opportunity to spin her in my arms. It's a pretense of romance. A moment of imagining she's mine. The villain doesn't get to keep the princess. Her dark hair flies around her, and she laughs. *Oomph.* She lands against my chest. I'm standing still in a ballroom full of movement. She's clasped to my body.

They've done something smoky to her eyes. They're more black than brown tonight. A galaxy inside this woman. A universe. I want to kiss her, but not here—in private. These people don't matter. I dip my head and press an almost-chaste kiss to her lips.

She doesn't return the kiss. "Is she still alive? You said it wouldn't be a sweet reunion, as if she's still alive. You must know that much. You must have checked."

A fire-burnished poker could not have burned me more. It steals my breath. "Yes. The last time I checked she was still alive. She started a new family."

I need her to kiss me back, so I bite her lower lip. She gasps into my mouth. That gives me the opening. I sweep my tongue against hers. A faint moan. It might as well be an orchestra, that's how keenly I hear the sound she makes. Her whole body sighs into my embrace.

Ruthless. That's what I am to distract her this way.

My head lifts. I study her half-closed eyes, her high cheekbones, her chin. It's like I'm looking at her for the very first time. Adding thirty years to her features. Comparing her to a woman on the train.

Shock tightens my hold on her arms, until she squirms.

Her eyes widen. "What's wrong?"

"Nothing," I say, but it's too damn late.

Suspicion makes her eyes glisten. "Who did you think was coming to get me after my father died? Why did you wait two weeks, Liam? Tell me the truth."

When you step on a land mine, you hold down the trigger. You can stand there as long as you want. Completely still. That's how long you stay alive. As soon as you move, the bomb goes off. "Your mother. I knew she was still alive. I thought she'd come for you when your father died."

A blast of both force and fire. She blinks. "The woman on the train. That was her?"

"We don't know that."

Emotions pass over her beautiful face—

heartbreak and confusion. Pain and a deep well of betrayal. That the woman who gave birth to her left her to that cold orphanage. That the woman had left her a long time before that. At least my mother escaped a living hell when she abandoned us. Samantha's mother doesn't have that excuse. I would kill to spare her this hurt. Ironic that I'm the one who caused it.

She pulls away from me. I catch her wrist. Disillusionment makes her eyes look wide open, broken so that I can see the tender space inside her. "I need to be alone," she says.

Yes, I understand. I hate it, but I understand. I've made an entire life so that I could be alone. If your own mother doesn't want you, how can you ever believe anyone else would? Safer to hold everyone at arm's length. Safer to flee the ballroom, tears in your eyes, dark curls flying behind her. It might not make sense to other people, but people who've been abandoned this way understand. It cracks the foundation of a person. It leaves a fissure that only deepens with time. I want to go after her, to insist that she accept comfort, to hold her down until she understands that she's worthy. Love doesn't really work like that. Nor is my comfort worth much, in the end. It's the princes of the world who can give her the security she really needs—the wholesome happy ending.

CHAPTER NINE

The piano was originally called the pianoforte because of its ability to play notes both quietly (piano) and loudly (forte). The harpsichords that came before were only able to play softly.

SAMANTHA

AWAY. I DON'T know where I'm running, except away.

When I'm far enough from the buzz of the crowd I turn down a hallway. At the end there are double doors that lead onto a patio. Do I want fresh air? No. There might be people outside.

Instead I duck into a dark room. My back to the wall, I heave deep breaths, struggling not to cry. I don't want her to have that power over me, this person who did not care enough to stay with me. Liam cares about me. I know that. He must be hurt by the way I left him standing there, but I couldn't bear the comfort of his embrace another second.

I press a hand to my stomach, where the bodice of the ballgown meets the wide skirts. Good luck. That's what the ladybug is supposed to mean. I'm not sure the symbolism applies.

Large shadows fill the room I'm in. My eyes adjust. Familiar shadows.

A laugh finds me. Fatalism. Is that what it's called? Of course I would end up in the music room, of all places. Definitely bad luck, but probably unavoidable. Instruments are the iron fillings, and I'm the magnet. They end up around me, no matter where I go.

It's a large music room, befitting the large chateau. There's a violin case next to a stand. The instrument inside is probably of good quality. Some violinists are particular about only playing their own instruments. I'm not usually, but the thought of playing *any* violin makes me cringe.

There was a grand piano in the ballroom, but there's an upright here. More modest. I sit down on the bench and run my fingers along the smooth curve of the lid. Do I dare play? I don't have permission but I can't really imagine Isa objecting.

Then again, it would be Fransisco who might.

I lift the lid. The white keys gleam in the low light. I touch the ivory lightly, not making a sound. It's like saying hello to the instrument. The instrument says hello back in indescribable ways, as if it's giving me permission to play. I'm still not sure I want to. That night, it was more than Liam getting shot. It was the death of a dream. It was the certainty that music would never have its way.

I press down the C at the center. Strong. Clear. Well-tuned, of course.

Another note. There's a feeling like relief, as if I've been holding on to bars above shark-infested waters. And suddenly I've let go. I'll be torn to bits but, in this moment, it feels too good to worry. My mind doesn't form the music. The music forms me. My fingers have no choice but to follow. The song starts quiet and careful, then grows louder, louder, louder. I sweep my hands across the keys in a complicated crescendo. God. *God.* My mother was alive this whole time. She didn't want me. *No one wants you.* Black and white blur together. I can't see the keys. A hot tear drops to the back of my hand. Even without my sight I can hit the notes unerringly. The final refrain.

And then silence in the room. I'm no longer alone here.

He crosses the room to stand behind me. "That was beautiful," he says, his voice low.

Not Liam. Alarm spikes through me before I

recognize the voice. Alexander Fox. Did he follow me here? I'm surprised Liam let him. The thought comes only after I realize Liam would have followed me too. I don't know how I'm sure, except that he knows I'm upset.

He wouldn't let me come to harm in my grief.

"What was it?" Alexander asks, sitting beside me on the small bench.

I'm immediately aware of his size, his physicality. He isn't as hard-hewn as Liam, but he's strong all the same. A stable kind of strength. The sort I could lean on, even though I sit very straight, not touching. "This? Nothing. A little something I made up."

Or is it? I'll never be able to trust my own mind. Is it something that I wrote? Is it something my father made me memorize? How depressing to realize that I'm not even safe in my head.

Alexander rests his right hand on the piano. His fingers look very strong compared to my slender ones. Darker, too, as if his skin has tanned from work outdoors instead of playing instruments inside. He plays a few notes that I had done, an echo, a callback. I give him a sideways glance. He has a decent ear, but then they would hardly put him in charge of the concert at Palais Garnier if he didn't.

I play a few more notes, a continuation. He pauses for only a beat before playing them back to me at a lower scale. It makes me laugh, so I play a more complicated arrangement for a longer beat.

"Ah, you surpass me without even breaking a sweat," he says, looking charmed.

My heart flutters at the look in his eyes—intense and a little romantic. It's enough to distract from the pain in my heart. The realization that I'm fully alone. Am I, though? There's a handsome man sitting on the piano bench with me. Someone who understands my passion for music the way someone else never could. The way Liam never could. The idea feels disloyal but still true.

I touch the keys without pressing them down. "What would you say if I never played the violin again? Would I still be Samantha Brooks? Or would I be someone else?"

His eyes search mine. Concern tightens his expression. "Is that what you want?"

What a funny idea. *Is that what you want?* My future has been foretold for so long I'm not even sure I know how to want. Unless base human desires count as wanting. I want to be held, to be kissed, to be safe. Is that what he means? The violin gives me none of those things—and all of them, because men are only in my life because of my skill.

Alexander's close enough that I can see the brown flecks in his eyes. Close enough I feel the warmth of his breath. "Stop me if you don't want this," he murmurs, before his lips glance mine.

There would be no time to stop him, but I don't really want to. Isn't that what human touch is about? Knowing that we aren't floating helplessly through space and time? His mouth is warm over mine, comforting. *This is courting*, I realize. He presses more firmly but doesn't put his tongue in my mouth. He doesn't grab my breast over my dress. This isn't about sex. It's about… affection.

He pulls back slightly, and I breathe in the moment between us.

My eyes open slowly. A light burns in his eyes, and I realize I've misread this. I've misread everything. Maybe it comes from growing up overprotected. What would have happened at a middle school dance? What would have happened if there'd been a boy's basement? Alexander feels lust, even if the only thing I feel for him is a kindness, a yearning. For what? For innocence.

"Did I move too fast?" he asks, his lids dropping low.

He respects me enough to wait. I don't want him to. *Prove that I can want someone else. Prove that I can desire another man.* I reach up to grasp his neck. He feels different here. Softer. His hair a little longer at the back, curling over his collar. He obeys my silent command, giving me a deeper kiss that steals my breath in its intimacy. His tongue touches mine in question. He tastes different.

He tastes *different*. As if there's one right way to taste. The Liam North flavor. The feel of his body. He's the standard by which I measure every other man. No one else will live up.

I tear myself away, breathing hard.

"Sorry," he says, a little breathless. "Sorry."

"You don't have anything to apologize for. I was the one who—" I was the one who wanted to see how fully my body had imprinted on Liam. Like those musicians who can only play one instrument. My particular instrument is hard and gruff and wounded, but it's *mine*.

Arousal makes Alexander more stern. More handsome. There is some woman who would swoon for him. That woman isn't me. "I'd like to see you again," he says. "Outside the concert."

My mouth opens. Nothing comes out. No polite refusals. No explanations.

He glances towards the door. "Are you thinking of Liam North?"

This is worse. Or maybe it's better. If he understands the way my heart is already claimed—

"I know he's your guardian," he says, his voice low as if imparting a secret. "And I see the way he looks at you. Some men think they can control you. He doesn't hurt you, does he?"

Oh God. "No. I promise, no."

"He's friends with Frans. I've heard the rumors about him."

The rumors about Fransisco? That makes me want to ask Isa whether she's okay. Maybe she needs help. Then again she seems happy enough. "He isn't dangerous, is he?"

A small laugh. "Every man is dangerous if he's threatened."

"Even you?"

"Even me." He says it solemnly, as if making a promise. "If you need to get away from him, I can make that happen. I have friends here in Paris who will help me. He has no legal hold on you anymore."

No legal hold on me. Something far more unbreakable. A hold on my heart.

"I'm not in trouble," I say, my voice as serious as Alexander's. Because it's not entirely the truth. I'm in danger from a thousand different sources.

From violence and from heartbreak. It's not because a man won't let go, though. It's because he won't hold on. "Thank you for your concern. Believe me, it means the world to know you'd do that, but I'm okay."

He composes a soft, quick ending to our playful music from before. "In that case, I should leave you to your solitude that I so rudely interrupted."

"I didn't mind," I say, repeating the new ending at a higher octave.

A bow doesn't detract from his open expression. "I'll see you at the theater?"

"For sure."

He pauses. "If you never played the violin again, I would say that we would definitely suffer a loss. From a professional standpoint I have to ask you to continue. As someone who admires you, I want you to do whatever you need."

In the silence after he goes, I look over at the violin.

I could play it now, before anyone else is here to listen. The ghostly imprint of bow and strings touches my fingertips. Silent strains sail through the air. A shiver runs down my spine. It's not that I'm apathetic. That would be easier to bear. My skill would at least carry me through a concert or two. It's more that I have a bone-deep repulsion. It's like asking me to step into boiling lava. My body shies away before my mind can even negotiate.

A coward. That's who stands up from the piano and leaves the room. Not strong enough to kiss a man who might actually build a relationship with me—one without guilt or sacrifice. Not strong enough to play the violin, the instrument my hands were born to know.

The hallway is as dark as I found it. As empty.

Except that the door to the balcony is open now. Was it closed before? I think so. A chill drifts down the darkened corridor. I take a step toward the end. There, to the side. A silhouette. I recognize him from behind. I could recognize him anywhere. He faces the grounds, his hands resting on the balcony, his shoulders broad, his hips lean. The tuxedo contours to his power, revealing its form.

Without really thinking it through I walk toward him. Then I set my hands on the cool stone beside his. "You could hear the piano inside."

And he would have had to pass us to get here. Which means he saw Alexander in there with me. Sitting beside me on the bench. Maybe even kissing me. And he didn't interrupt us?

"It sounded like you made a friend."

A friend. "I'm surprised you didn't come in."

"The way I did during the dance? It isn't right for me to stop you. If you want a man like him…" He looks away. "He's the kind of man you're going to end up with."

My eyes narrow. He no longer bothers saying that I *should* end up with a man like Alexander. Instead he thinks I will. Like it's inevitable. Like I have no choice in the matter. Even if I married him, even if I had three children, he would always assume I'd leave—the way his mother did.

There's no convincing him, I realize with a sinking feeling in my stomach.

The past has written too deeply into his skin. It made him bleed and left the scars in the shape of the words, proving he'll always be abandoned by those he loves.

"You let him kiss me?"

Liam flinches. He could not know what happened for sure, but he meant to let me. "It's your choice."

"You would have let him make love to me on that piano bench, is that right?"

A low growl escapes him. "Yes."

"If he had flipped up my skirt and touched

me the way you touch me. If he made me come so hard that I called out his name." I make my voice breathless and high. "*Alexander. Yes.*"

Liam backs me against the tall stone railing. "Don't push me."

"If you didn't want to hear it, why wait here? Why torture yourself?"

A pleading look in his green eyes. "That's all I know how to do."

"I'm tired of being your punishment, Liam North. Make me something else. Show me what it would be like if you took what you wanted, no guilt, no regrets. If you did anything to me. No restraint."

His expression turns hard. "You don't—"

I slap him. I don't know why I do. I'm not really angry at him; it's more that I'm desperate. Being soft hasn't done enough. This is a man who works out on a daily basis in ways that would break most men. He doesn't even feel the softness.

I want a reaction from him—and he gives me one.

His fist captures me wrist. Then my hand's behind my back. Both of my arms are pinned behind me. The lace overlay with its black dots flutters in the breeze—my wings. He uses them to tie a knot. Netting traps my wrists behind me and pushes my breasts forward.

"You said you wouldn't touch me until I played the violin."

"Tell me to stop."

Please don't stop. "I did play the piano, though."

A short laugh. "Will we call this a reward? Or a punishment?"

"I don't know." The air feels thin now. My breath comes faster. The bodice that lifted and constrained my breasts now struggles to hold me.

"This is what I'd do," Liam says, sounding casual. "If I could do anything to your body, without guilt, without regret, without worrying about damaging you, I would keep you tied up. So I could touch you whenever I wanted, however I wanted."

The words make my thighs clench together.

He studies my breasts, the way they swell over the top of the red satin. I'm not a voluptuous woman, but I might be Venus from the concentration he gives them. His fingers feather over my breast, his thumb fanning my nipple through the bodice. Sparks of pleasure awaken every dormant impulse. The moment in Nantes was more battle than sensual dance. The bathroom on the train an illicit snapshot. This balcony extends a thousand years into the future. A thousand years into the past. There's nothing else except endless decadence.

"I might have felt guilty for this," he says, dipping two fingers between my skin and satin. They find my nipple in an indelicate movement, holding the nub between them. *Squeeze.* My breath catches. "You said not to feel any guilt. Right?"

"Right." My voice trembles as he tugs down the dress, exposing my breasts to the night air. Anyone could see us. If they walked down the hallway. If they strolled along the darkening lawn.

He frames my breasts, making them look even smaller. The scarred and weather-tanned skin of his fingers, the coarse hair on the back of his hand, it contrasts sharply with pale smoothness. Thumb and forefinger grasp my nipple without the dress to limit him. He tugs hard enough to make me yelp. The sensation fires straight to my center, turning my sex liquid.

"No regrets," he says, his voice almost regretful. As if he would like to feel bad about the small pain he caused me, but he simply cannot. It wouldn't be polite at this point, his tone implies. Everything about his demeanor speaks of formality. Which makes the way he licks his thumb more explicit.

The damp tip makes me shiver.

"What if someone—what if someone comes?"

A low laugh. "Are you worried you will? Or worried you won't?"

My cheeks flush. "Someone else. If they see us…"

"You're a performer," he says, his tone musing. "They'll see you performing."

"Not like this." My voice squeaks at the end, because he bends to flick my nipple with his tongue. Such a small gesture. Such a soft touch, but it feels sharp. A hundred knives couldn't shock me more.

"No, you'd prefer to play the violin. Or would you? It's an Amati they have in the music room. You wouldn't know because you couldn't even bring yourself to open the case."

My cheeks warm. This man has seen me at my lowest. In an orphanage. Afraid. Alone. He's never seen me unable to play the violin, though. Until now. "Alexander said I should do what I want."

"Alexander wants to fuck you."

I flinch at the crude words. Of course I've heard the word *fuck* before. You don't grow up on a compound full of ex-military mercenaries without hearing your share of them. Liam doesn't use them too often. Not around me, anyway. "You don't know that."

"I do know that, because every man in that ballroom wanted to fuck you. When you walked down the stairs, when you smiled at those old fuckers in tuxedos, they were thinking about how you'd look on your back, your legs spread wide for them."

The words should be offensive. They *are* offensive, but a strange fever has taken hold of me. I find it exciting that so many men would want me. I don't know if it's true or not, but it feels true. The dress has turned me into a siren. I've had admiration from grown men for my talent since I was a child. This is different. This is desire.

Liam bites down gently on my nipple, making me squirm. "I wouldn't normally explain that, but it's the same thing I thought about you."

"Are you going to... you know?"

He smiles, though it's not really with humor. It's more like he's mocking himself. "Am I going to fuck a young woman who can't even bring herself to say the words? I wouldn't have, but you don't want me to feel guilt. You don't want me to feel regret."

He makes no move to lift my skirts or to open

his pants. I'm standing in front of him like a sacrificial offering, my hands tied behind my back, my breasts bared, and all he does is touch. Each move is careful, pausing for… what? For me to say no? He thinks I'm going to give up. He thinks I'm going to cry off. God, he still thinks I'm going to leave. This whole thing is a challenge. Maybe I'm the one who issued it when I pretended to moan Alexander's name. Anything less than completion won't satisfy me now. Not only the kind he gave me by the ocean. He made me come but left himself unfinished. He left himself invulnerable.

"Does guilt own you that much?" I ask, taunting. "Does regret? You talk a good game."

He looked half-feral most of the days in the small town, a few days' growth on his jaw, his hair mussed by the ocean breeze. Now he looks smooth. Polished. His square jaw freshly shaven. His hair ruthlessly styled so it will fit in with the crowd. He probably thinks he's anonymous as he walks through the ballroom. As if every woman doesn't turn her head to watch him from behind.

"You own me," he says, his voice low. It carries on the wind. Green eyes flash—not with guilt or regret. They flash with a kind of resignation.

It isn't a pleasure, this possession I have of

him. But it's real.

"Alexander," I say, not loud enough to really reach the ballroom. I pretend to call for some other lover. Someone who will finish what Liam started.

A real laugh then, and it's worth it. Whatever happens next, whatever sin he visits on my body will be worth it to see the genuine way he throws back his head. "Quiet now, Ms. Brooks. Let's see if we can put that pretty mouth to better use."

CHAPTER TEN

Sonatas were at first written mainly for the violin. Over time a binary form emerged, with most modern sonatas featuring both a violin and a piano.

LIAM

FOLDED OVER, MY tux jacket provides little support from the marble floor. Her dress will probably shield her better. Regardless, she may end up with bruises on her knees. She may be the one filled with regret at the end of the night, but I won't deny her. I can't deny her. I wasn't lying before—she owns me.

"There was something else," I say, helping her kneel, every movement overly courteous, as if I'm being the consummate gentleman instead of a bastard. "Something else you didn't want me to use."

Her eyes shine with anticipation as she looks up at me. And fear. Not too much of it, but enough. I have never been interested in Fransisco's kinky games, but I understand the edge of uncertainty and how it can sharpen lust to a spear. "Restraint."

"That was it. Restraint. You don't want me to use any?"

She's trembling, whether from the fear or the cold I don't know.

God help me, I don't even care. Desire beats a tribal chant in my head. To take her. To claim her. To stretch her with my body so she always remembers who was inside her.

Her lids drop to her cheeks. "Maybe a little bit of restraint."

"Don't back down now." I brush my knuckles against her cheek. "Not when you're being so brave. Isn't that what you want? Something rough to remember me by?"

She looks up, her eyes flashing. There's no demure young woman now. Even on her knees she looks powerful. "That's what it would take, is that it? Any woman would have to be brave to accept who you really are? Fine, then. Call me brave."

I don't know what she means about any woman. I only want her. My dick doesn't care what she's talking about. It likes her brave and powerful. It likes her on her knees.

From this position I can see the crown of her

head and the silhouette of her face. I can see her breasts in their glory, framed by a wide spill of red silk around her. It's the sight a man needs for a complete life. I could die having known this pleasure, even before her mouth touches me.

I open my pants with unsteady hands. Relief. It's short-lived relief. Even freed from my briefs my cock throbs in hungry pulses. The night air might as well be sandpaper. Anything but her body will be painful. Part of me still expects her to turn her face away. It's an ugly sight, the red, veined cock. An intimidating one, especially considering her hands are still tied behind her back. She's completely at my mercy. If I shove too far, too fast, if I push down her throat, she can't stop me.

No restraint.

Maybe a little bit of restraint.

She's smart to temper the command. I'll try to find a little bit of restraint. Though it will be hard when her lips are so full, so plump. Her tongue flicks out, a flash of pink, before it retreats.

I press my cock to her lips. She doesn't open for me. No, she wants me to work for it. To fight her. That only makes me harder, and I grasp her neck, tilting back her head. She opens on a gasp, and I use the opportunity to press inside.

Wetness. Heat. Velvet. It takes herculean effort to continue standing under the onslaught of her mouth. Christ. I push inside her, a little too far, a little too fast—exactly what she was asking for, begging for. She wants to be a little afraid tonight.

Her tongue rolls around the head, and I curse under my breath. "You're so fucking beautiful, Samantha. So fucking perfect. I'll never forget you like this."

The flash of anger again. She wants me to believe she'll stay by my side forever. I might as well believe in fairies and dragons and magic. There isn't forever for us. A graze of her teeth to the underside of my cock. My balls tighten in instinctive warning. That's her punishment for my lack of faith. It should be terrible, but instead I laugh towards the moon. Sex has been a form of physical relief for so long. Like running twenty miles until I collapse. The euphoria comes because it's over. It's always been different with her. More meaningful. More sweet. Only now has she learned to make it… fun. Playful. It's a game where the stakes are more than her body. More than her heart. They might even be her future.

From somewhere in the house a large grandfather clock chimes ten times.

Ten o'clock. Have the guests noticed she's

missing from the ballroom? It's large enough that they may not. Between the dance floor and the refreshments there's enough places she could be not to think she left completely. There are even private sitting rooms for those who want smaller groups. Or parties of two. The doors can be closed. Locked.

The equivalent of a sock on the knob.

We're not supposed to be down this hallway. Not supposed to be fucking on the balcony, but I don't think Frans will mind. "Stay still," I tell her, touching her jaw so she understands. "I want to fuck your mouth. It's different than sucking me."

Her eyes look impossibly wide as she looks up at me, like she's some anime drawing instead of a flesh and blood woman. The sensation around my cock leaves no doubt as to her composition. The slide of her tongue turns my cock to stone. I thrust my hips toward her. A rude gesture. Unworthy of her. It's what I want to do to her every time I look at her lips, so I indulge myself. *No restraint.* I find a steady rhythm, allowing her to suck in breaths between my thrusts.

Christ, I want to come down her throat.

No. I want to make this last forever.

It's too good to decide. Too perfect to last.

Over the eddies of pure sensation I feel the

buzz on my watch. It's time to do a security check. That takes precedent over ecstasy. Only, I can't push her away from my cock. Self-discipline evaporates under the onslaught of her agile little tongue.

"Report," I say into my watch. "Webb."

"Clear."

Samantha looks up at me, pure mischief in her eyes. A sweep around the crown of my cock. A broad lick over the head. My knees almost buckle. "Rogers," I grind out.

"Clear."

I warned them when I followed Samantha and that Alexander not to let anyone into the hallway. And to keep the south side of the lawn empty. No one's going to see Samantha's breasts except for me, but she doesn't know that. The excitement makes her chest rise and fall in rapid rhythm. The sight of her plump tits makes my mouth water.

"North."

"Clear," he says in a drawl that sounds knowing.

"Your command," I say, flipping my connection to *off*.

The static goes quiet. My heartbeat thuds so loud I'm sure the birds and the crickets in the trees around the house can hear it. Hoarse curse words escape me on every thrust. Uneven movements take my hips. I'm so close to coming I feel an early spurt come from the tip. Her eyes widen, but she swallows it down like a good girl. *Fuck. So good. Yes.*

It's a physical pain to pull out of her mouth. Her jaw must be sore, but I don't give her a break. Instead I drag her up and kiss her, rubbing my tongue along hers, thanking her, worshipping her the only way I know how.

The lace doesn't want to untie. I rip it apart to free her hands. She gasps in surprise. Maybe dismay over the gown. I'll buy her another one. I'll buy her fifty of them. I spin her around. She grabs the wide stone balcony to catch herself. That's all the warning I give her before I reach down to flip up her skirts. Ah. God. Her ass looks like a pale peach heart framed by the piles of red satin. I pull down her black lace panties so they trap her ankles in place. Then I plunge inside her burning heat, groaning with the exquisite pleasure of it, only the smallest part of me worried about how quickly I stretched her tender skin. She's gone stock-still. Her knuckles turn white where she clutches the balustrade. She's wet enough, almost dripping down her legs, but that doesn't mean she was ready for me. I should have fingered her first. I should have tongued her instead of fucking her as hard and as fast as I would my fist. There's no pulling out of this heaven. All I can do is reach around to tap her clit. She sucks in a breath when I find it. There's no soft tease this time. No slow climb. I rub firmly across it, in a way that might actually hurt, but it will also hurl her over the other side. Her climax rises fast and slams into her. She ripples around my cock, milking me, forcing my own orgasm in wild, reckless pulses against her innermost muscles.

The aftermath comes to me in slow, drifting notes. It takes me a while to realize I'm crushing her against the stone. Longer to know that my come drips down her leg. Guilt. Regret. The things she didn't want me to feel, except I can't stop being myself—not even for the woman I love.

I press a kiss to her naked shoulder. "Did I hurt you?"

She doesn't answer. Panic rises in my throat. I spin her around to look at her face. She looks... frantic. Her cheeks are flushed. Something glazes her eyes. Tears? Arousal? I can't deny that she still looks turned on, a woman well-fucked and ready for more. Desperate for it.

"You came, didn't you?" I felt the clench of

her pussy around me.

Her teeth are chattering. "I did. I did, but—"

But there's more pressure built inside. It needs release. I pull her into my arms and drift into the corner of the balcony, where ivy gives us some cover from the stars. "Shhh," I say, pressing an endless kiss to her crown. "I'll make it better. Let me, let me. Relax, little prodigy."

I rub her clit nice and slow this time, despite the urgent way she hitches her hips. It's more of a soothing caress than an inciting one. She leans into my body, searching, searching. Her whole body goes rigid. She comes with a gush of warmth on my fingers, enough to make my cock throb awake again.

She leans her head back against the stone façade. Her eyes are closed. The urgency is gone, but the melancholy rises to the surface. It was too much for her. Maybe not too much for her body, but for her emotions, especially considering what she learned about her mother tonight. I would beat myself up for it, but self-recrimination takes a back seat to my concern for her. I tug her dress up to cover her breasts and smooth the skirt down. Except for the wild riot of curls around her shoulders, you might not know she's just been fucked hard. Even so, there's no way she's going back to the ballroom. I dust off my tux jacket from the marble floor and throw it over her shoulders.

Her lids rise. She looks dazed. The lights are too dim, like stars a hundred million miles away. It makes worry beat against my ribs. Finally she focuses on me. "Alexander would have never done it like that."

I shake my head.

"I liked it," she says, her voice wobbling at the end.

Then she bursts out crying. It's not a soft cry. Not a silent one. The sobs are enough to wrack her body. An earthquake in human form. She cries like she's lost everything in the world, the way a young girl might cry in an orphanage— except she'd been dry eyed all those years ago.

I hold her close to my body, knowing it's a thin comfort I offer, feeling her thinness, her frailty, the breakable thread of her as she pours her grief into my chest.

CHAPTER ELEVEN

The main groups of singing insects are cicadas, grasshoppers,
locusts and crickets. Each species produces a distinctive sound.
In almost all cases, only the males sing.

BETHANY

I'M DANCING WITH a vicomte when Alexander Fox finds me.

He stands against the wall, his expression indicating that it's time. He's always been charming and respectful to me. It makes me wonder what would have happened if his United States counterparts had been that way. Without the reality show or the elaborate staging, would we have been so vulnerable? Would the shooting have happened? The shot did more than blast through Liam North's body. Layers of muscle and bone. One of the strongest men I've ever met. It took him down, because in the end he's still a man—not a god. It shook more than him, because the tour ended. I know I'm not the only one who's nervous about getting back on a stage.

SONATA

Performers are a suspicious lot. Maybe the tour
shouldn't have been resurrected. Maybe it should
have ended that day in New York City, even if
that feels like defeat.

The song ends, and the vicomte twirls me
around with a flourish. He's twice my age, but
that sort of thing doesn't matter to these people.
My skin color matters, though. Enough to make
me wonder if he's giving me that gallant smile
because he's interested in me—or because he
thinks I'll give him a quick fuck in the bathroom.
Even rich people like quickies.

Well, it doesn't matter what he wants from
me. I'm here to do a job. It's best to begin before
the nerves paralyze me completely. Performers are
superstitious, but I come from New Orleans. I
threw salt over my shoulder and would hang
garlic over my bed since I was a little girl. My
mind knows that the shooting happened because
Samantha's father was in business with bad
people. The ancient part of my mind wonders if
standing on a stage with her again is a good idea.

It takes some searching to find Romeo. I have
to ask for the man with broad shoulders and an
earring in his left ear. It makes him look vaguely
like a pirate. Eventually I stumble across a row of
closed doors. It's like a bad game show, where I'm

probably going to end up embarrassed.

The first door opens to reveal three people engaged in a very acrobatic arrangement. It could easily be something on the floor of Cirque du Monde—clothed, of course. I murmur a quick apology and shut the door, even though I don't think they noticed me.

The second door reveals a woman being pleasured by a man who must be half her age. There's a stark enough difference that I wonder whether she's the aristocracy in this relationship.

The third door finally reveals two men, their clothes half-shed across the sitting room. Romeo has the man backed up against a window ledge. They're making out with mouths clashing, hands clenched. I clear my throat. "Romeo," I whisper. And then louder, "Romeo!"

I wouldn't normally interrupt him, except that we promised to do this small performance. It felt like a safe way to ease back into dancing. It's been hard to start after the shooting.

He tears himself away with clear reluctance. I recognize the word he uses in Spanish, even though it's slang and extremely rude. "Tell them to wait."

"They're signing our checks, so no, I'm not going to tell them that."

With a groan, he steps back. "Wait here," he says gruffly.

"I'm sorry," I tell the anonymous other person. I have no intention of knowing who it is—and certainly wouldn't mind if Romeo played with any of the guests. Recognition makes me do a double take. I manage a weak smile at the man before Romeo reaches the door.

"A servant?" I hiss when he's outside. "I don't think Frans would—"

"Oh, he'd rather I fuck one of his fancy counts or barons? Like I'm some kind of performing monkey. Dance when he wants. Suck dick when he wants."

A flinch. "You're going to get him in trouble."

"Don't worry about him. Besides, you're the one making sex eyes at the man who's probably going to get all of us killed."

Anger lances through me. Along with worry. "I don't make sex eyes at anyone, thank you very much. And what do you mean, he'll get us killed?"

"That's what they're trying to do. You didn't know? That's the purpose of this concert. To draw out whoever was after Samantha in New York."

We reach the top of the stairs, and I manage a

bright smile despite my concern. I have a long history of giving a fake façade. Most people think I'm happy and calm. They think I'm at peace no matter what turmoil's inside me. Romeo holds his arm out, and I place my hand in it. He's wearing a black costume tuxedo with a yellow cumberbund. He's the worker bee. I'm the queen. We pass by the man in question—Joshua North. His green eyes take me in with cool appraisal. Of everyone in the room, he doesn't look fooled. He knows I'm worried. Then again, that's only fair. Because he also knows why.

We take our places in the center of the ballroom. A hush falls over the crowd. The quartet already knows the piece we need. Romeo does a wide sweeping step, his form utter perfection. Like me, he knows how to fake it. No matter his desire for the servant or his worry over the concert. We're like the musicians on the Titanic. We continue playing even when the ship goes down. He lifts me up, and I make my circle around the hive. I'm the queen of all I survey, even if I can never leave my post. The dance passes without flaw. Perfect technique. Endless practice will do that. I'm lucky that my partner has the same devotion to practice as me. We end with a bow and curtsey. The whole room erupts into applause. So much praise. Wonder. They're easily pleased once plied with champagne. Only one man in the room doesn't clap. He watches me instead, his green gaze troubled, as if he's only now felt the water at his ankles, only now realized the ship we're on is sinking.

JOSH

I SHOULD HAVE done this yesterday but I stayed in Paris to watch Bethany's performance last night. So do otherwise ordinary men turn into fools for women. Not women, plural. A single woman. She had been incandescent in the center of that ballroom. Utterly regal. Unfortunately, she's also very much off-limits. The only way I know how to be with a woman is to fuck. Hard. Fast. And then leave. For reasons I haven't quite deciphered, I don't want to do that with her.

After ten hours of flights to our compound in Texas and ten hours of flights back, I have the violin in hand. I would give Samantha a hard time about needing this *particular* violin, except I understand it. I like my particular gun. I can use another one in a pinch, but there's something about mine that fits better in my hand, that aims better, that shoots better. She probably wouldn't appreciate the comparison.

A knock on the apartments next to hers. I don't wait for an answer, because there are some benefits to being a younger brother—and being an annoying shit is one of them. I push open the door. Liam stands at the window, holding a cup of coffee. He looks like he's thinking deep thoughts. Instead he's probably calculating whether there are any openings in the chateau's security. There aren't.

"You're welcome," I say, setting the violin down on the sofa. When wood and catgut goes for a couple million dollars, it gets to sit on cushions instead of a table.

He glances at the case, not looking particularly grateful. "Thank you."

I throw myself onto an armchair, wincing a little at how it creaks. Damn antique furniture isn't made to hold a man and his six-pack. "I should have brought it to her, so I could at least enjoy the way she freaks out and starts petting it like it's a kitten."

Liam looks out the window some more.

Suspicion makes me sit up straighter. More creaking. Goddamn. "Unless you think she won't be happy to see the violin? It's weird she didn't mind it more, not being able to play."

"She's a violinist."

That's what he said in that tiny town near Nantes. The more he says it, the more I wonder if something has changed. That girl was all about her violin. When he first adopted her, I barely heard her speak, but she could damn well play. All night. All day. I ended up moving my bedroom across the compound so I could actually sleep. "She better be, considering there are two thousand rich-ass French people lining up to watch her play next week."

He doesn't respond, which probably means he's really worried.

I study his profile, wondering when the hell he turned into an old man. I suppose if he's old then I am, too. "How old are you, now? Thirty-six? Thirty-seven?"

"Thirty-five."

"You act like a monk."

He snorts, which probably alludes to his bad, bad thoughts about sweet little Samantha. Real monks probably have worse thoughts. And walk around with erections all day. Why else wear a robe? "They're going to make a move on her during the concert."

"Of course they are. That's the whole point."

"I need you to be careful."

That makes me pause. The plan is that he'll provide close cover to Samantha. Because, let's face it, it's not like he could leave her side anyway. I'll be the one leading the team to capture whoever's in the audience. We have men placed strategically throughout the theatre. It took some negotiating to place that number, considering how many euros each seat is going for. They'll probably send more than one person this time. It's my job to take them down. I wouldn't expect Liam to worry about me. "You know I can take care of myself," I say lightly.

His expression darkens. "I know. You've been doing it long enough."

The reference hangs in the air between us, the past real enough I can smell the sweet grass and rotting garbage. "I don't blame you for leaving. Hell, I'd have happily left you behind if I could have."

"No," he says thoughtfully. "I don't think so. You were always the most loyal."

That makes me laugh. "Jesus. Does she have your brain fucked up from all the sex?"

"Don't talk about her that way."

"It was a bad scene." That's really an understatement. Our father had been a crazy fucker who thought his children were the devil, spawn of the wife who left him. He was the hardest on Liam. "If I blame anyone it was the adults who could have stopped it."

"There was the teacher who tried."

"Those trash bags filled with our dirty shit." I shake my head. We had been moved to a temporary foster home, three boys who barely took baths or knew how to communicate without our fists. The foster mother had been horrified. The foster father had been disgusted.

"And then dear old dad killed her cat. It was only a matter of time after that."

"Is that what happened? I didn't remember."

Liam looks at me, pain in his dark green eyes. "Probably because you were busy being traumatized at the bottom of that goddamn well."

I shift, uncomfortable that he's brought it up after all this time. Our dad had dropped me down there. At least I'd been old enough to land on my feet. When he'd tossed Elijah down after me, it was pure fucking luck that I managed to catch him. Then I held him up until my arms were shaking, made of jelly, trying to keep him out of the sick water, trying to ignore the things that slithered in it. "What brought this up?" I ask, standing to get rid of the memories—slick, damp, cold. "Some things are better left in the past."

"Most things are. The past has a way of catching up."

"Very poetic."

"Just take care of yourself, okay? I couldn't protect you then. I failed you then, but I don't want to see you die. Not even for Samantha."

"I don't plan to die for Samantha," I say with a laugh, even though it's not precisely true. I've been waiting to die for a long time. It may as well be for something that would bring my brother peace.

CHAPTER TWELVE

In England, Henry VIII ordered the licensing of minstrels and players. The punishment for non-compliance was to be whipped.

LIAM

PART OF ME thinks that if she only sees the violin, touches it, plays it, it will all rush back to her. The other part of me knows that won't happen.

I carry the case into her rooms and set it down on the bed. She pulls the blanket up around her. I might have set down a live snake on the bedspread, that's how horrified she looks. "What is that?"

"You know what it is." I turn to the small wet bar in her room and pour two fingers of whiskey. Something to loosen the grip her fear has on her.

She swallows it and coughs. "It's late."

"Not too late to play. I remember when I used to have to pry the bow from your hand and send you to bed, because you'd have played straight until dawn."

"That was a long time ago. I was young and stupid."

"You were young and scared." Scared of me, which felt terrible. And deserved. She didn't know me. Didn't know what I was capable of. The truth is—she's still young and scared.

I was old, like my brother said. Old enough that I had no business touching her. Definitely no business sitting on her bed, not that it stopped me. I put my hand on her knee. "Better that you get it over with now. Only the first time will hurt. It'll get easier after that."

She manages a wan smile. "Are you taking my virginity?"

The question is meant as a joke. It still sends a wildfire through my blood. I remember how tight she was the first time, the way she squirmed for relief. The way I stretched her untried muscles until she had no choice but to surrender. "Something short and simple. Something to ease you into it."

"I told you I don't want to play."

"Then you should have taken Alexander up on his offer. He would no doubt let you lead him wherever you wanted. Instead you came outside the balcony." I'll remember that night until my last breath. My gratitude over her sweet submission isn't going to make me stop, though.

Anger flashes across her face. Fear. Guilt. "You're being strict for no reason. It's late at night. I don't want to play right now. Why can't you accept that?"

"Play me a chord, Samantha."

"No."

"Play me a chord and I'll leave you alone." That's not how I want this night to end, but if it's necessary I'll go back to my room alone and keep my fist company.

"Stop it."

The gunshot at Carnegie Hall did this to her.

She was playing when it went off. I almost died, and somehow, somehow, that matters to her. Her psyche drew a straight line between her playing and my death. I've seen it a thousand times with soldiers well trained for the physical and mental strains of warfare. She could no sooner pick up the bow and press it to the strings than she could pick up a gun and shoot me.

"Nothing bad will happen," I say gently. "I swear to you."

Her eyes flash with panic. "You don't know that. You don't know anything. I don't want to play the violin anymore, did you think of that?

I'm not afraid. I just don't like it."

I open the case. "You can play a song you don't like."

She flinches back from the open case. It's a beautiful violin. I know that mostly because I've seen her expression when she gazes at it, her expression of ecstasy when she plays. "Stop."

It feels like it weighs nothing when I pick it up. Insane to think it can fill an entire theater with its sound. Only in the hands of the right person, however. Like her. "You're a violinist."

"I'm not. That's just what you want me to be."

I run my thumb along the strings. "Is it? That's an interesting thought. Would I have fallen in love with you if you had never played a note? Would I have taken your virginity?"

"No." She clasps the idea close. "You wouldn't have. That's all you want. You don't care about *me*. So go find someone else to play your violin."

"Now it's my violin? I don't think so. It's yours." I hold it out for her. Her talent doesn't define her, but I won't let her fear define her either. "That bedpost is solid wood. Go ahead and smash it. There won't be anything to play then."

Her eyes narrow with suspicion.

She might wonder if I'd snatch it back from her if it seemed like she was going to break it. Maybe I will. There isn't a parenting guide for what to do when your child prodigy decides to stop playing out of mortal fear. If she had lost interest, I would have let it go. But I won't let the men who terrorized her take it away from her. I won't let her father do this from the grave.

"The violin is stronger than it looks," I offer. "You'll have to pull it back like a baseball bat. Really put your shoulder into it if you want it to shatter. It should at least be satisfying."

"It cost like two million dollars," she says, her fingers trembling as she reaches for the neck. I'm not sure whether she's thinking about breaking it or thinking about saving it from my violent words.

It actually cost more than that. "It doesn't matter, does it?"

"This is crazy. I don't have to smash it. I just have to *not* play."

I pretend to consider that. "No, I think you have to smash it. Otherwise I'll never leave it alone. I'll just be here insisting that you play me a song, a chord, a single note."

"Fine." She grasps the violin in her fist and stands beside the bed. A baseball bat. She's clearly never held one, but she gives it her best shot, aiming toward the thick post that frames the bed. "You want me to ruin this? You want me to destroy a precious violin? I'll do it."

How much is it worth? More than millions of dollars. It's worth her talent. Her heart. Watching her destroy it may destroy me—but I can't force her to play. "If you want to."

"I do. I do." She pulls the violin high behind her shoulder. Emotion rises in the air around us like a fog. I can barely see her for the pain that surrounds her. She bares her teeth in an imitation of ferocity. It looks more like grief. "I really, really do."

She stands there vibrating with her fear and her desire. Her hurt. She's like a string on that violin she holds, playing a long, heartrending note. It seems inevitable that she'll smash it against the bed. And probably regret it afterward.

Play the violin, I think. *Let yourself have this.*

The violin begins its downward arc. She lets it go at the last minute, and it flies through the air, landing harmlessly on the plush bed. A discordant sound erupts and then becomes muffled.

Samantha crumples on the rug, her face buried in her hands. Her shoulders shake with the violence of what she almost did—even though she still hasn't played. I lose the heart to force her to play. *You're being strict for no reason.* There is a reason, the most important one. For her happiness. I gather her in my arms for a different reason. My love for her.

We're done for the day.

SAMANTHA

THE NEXT MORNING my eyes feel swollen and gritty, but in the mirror I look pretty normal. My throat feels sore as if I screamed for hours instead of cried. I throw on a plain black tank top and jeans. Downstairs in the breakfast room I find a long buffet and a mostly empty table. Only one person sits there with coffee. Liam glances at me with alert green eyes. "Are you feeling okay this morning?"

He feels guilty for last night. Normally his guilt frustrates me. Today, I'll accept it. I'm still a little upset at him for forcing the issue. And perversely upset that he didn't force it all the way—so that I would have played. The violin sits in its case in my room. Not played. Not broken. A stalemate.

"Yes," I say, pulling a croissant onto a plate. "I was wondering if we could see the Eiffel Tower.

And whatever else there is to see in Paris. I've been here before but—"

"Not sightseeing."

He knows the way my father traveled. In places that cost more than we could afford, while I was carted around like baggage that required food and water. There were no museums or tourist places. "When I performed at the Palais Garnier that was the only place I went."

Which is dangerously close to what this visit might be like.

I know the reasons are completely different. My father didn't care about me enough to take me places. Liam cares too much to let me go out unguarded. The irony is that the result is the same. I'm trapped in this beautiful place I didn't choose.

Liam takes a sip of coffee. He's silent while I eat my croissant. He'll make some excuse. He'll say he has no choice. He'll say—"The Eiffel Tower. Okay. Where else? I'll take you."

My heart stops. "You will?"

"Unless you'd rather go with someone else. We could ask Bethany or—"

"No." I circle the table in my excitement and press a kiss on his cheek. He couldn't look more surprised if I had slapped him. In fact, he did look less surprised when I did that. "I want to go with you."

A black SUV appears in front of the chateau in an hour. One of the men I know from North Security drives. It leaves us at a long stretch of grass framed by tulips. The Eiffel Tower rises above lush green trees. I cast a sideways glance at Liam, wondering if he's immune to the romance of the place. It floats in the air around us. God, the sky is so blue. He looks stern and uncompromising. The typical Liam face. When he looks at me, I see that he's affected after all. Green eyes burn with a poignant knowledge. That we're here in this city. That we don't belong—but that there is no requirement to love. No barriers in this particular city. Society's rules have no jurisdiction here.

"Let's go up," he says, pointing the way to the line. What an ordinary thing to do with the man you love. That's what I want right now. What I need. An ordinary life. Even my heartbeat *thump thump thumps* in a black case in my room at the chateau.

He arranges a special tour of Notre-Dame even though it's closed to visitors, undergoing repairs. I walk beside the elaborate, colorful stained glass windows. I walk beside the confessionals.

A low bench lined with red leather and padding provides a place to pray. I light a candle and kneel. It reminds me of the time I knelt in front of Liam on the balcony on a different type of red fabric. Blasphemy, considering what I did to his body that night. What he did to mine. The same. It's the same anyway, the prayer that I make. For his safety. For mine.

That against the odds, we can both find it together.

CHAPTER THIRTEEN

The earliest form of musical notation can be found in a cuneiform tablet that was created in Babylonia, where Iraq is today, in 1400 BC.

SAMANTHA

IT'S WHEN WE'RE leaving Notre Dame that I spy the words *Shakespeare and Company.* Something about the familiarity makes me pause. That's when I realize. "The tote bag," I say, feeling faint. My stomach turns over. That my mother was only inches away from me. That she touched me, wiping the hot tea from my body, when I had no idea who she was, makes me feel strange. It's like someone walking on your grave—a sensation that you should never be aware of.

Liam squeezes my hand. "Let's go. We can visit the Louvre."

It's tempting. You don't spend a lifetime pursuing classical music without also acquiring a taste for classical art. The portrayals of instruments alone would be enthralling. "What is that place?"

"A bookstore." He pauses. "We asked around. She wasn't seen."

Of course they would have pursued that lead before I even thought of it. That's how Liam and Josh work, analyzing threats and subduing them. I suppose that means my mother is a threat. "I'd like to go inside."

Another hesitation. Longer this time. "I'm not sure that's a good idea."

"You won't stop me." Part of growing up means making my own decisions. It means walking into a place that may only cause me emotional pain. Whether as my guardian or my lover, Liam can't protect me from that.

He looks resigned. "A short visit."

A woman recites poetry using very sexual and explicit words to describe female anatomy. She stands in front of an upturned straw hat, collecting euros, much the way a street musician would do. An antique-looking suitcase sits open by the entrance, containing books wrapped in brown paper with descriptions. No book covers or titles to sway the buyer.

I swerve toward a shop next door that contains rare books. The scent of dust and decay assails me, but there's something distinguished about it. Old knowledge. Hope. I touch the spine of some of the books, wondering how many came before me. A case in the far corner catches my attention. Clouds obscure the glass. My heart soars when I recognize the signature. A letter written by Claude Debussy, the paper worn and brown, the script long and smudged. An autographed program from a concert in 1913.

A musical manuscript, undated, in Debussy's own hand.

He was a prodigy like me. He made his concert debut at age 10 here in Paris. *Violin Sonata No. 1*, says a placard next to the yellowed paper, along with a very high price tag.

I find myself bouncing on my toes as I peer into the case. The notes and scribbles in the margin—written in his own hand! The creases from where he might have folded it for keeping in his pocket. I'm one foot away from something he touched, only the length of the case separating us.

"Do you want it?" Liam says, his voice low beside me.

I jump and whirl, as if I've been caught touching something in a museum. "No."

"You do." He looks amused. "You can have it. You don't need my permission. There's money sitting in a bank account with your name on it, from the tour."

"Really?" Of course I knew I got paid for doing the tour. Though any thoughts of practical considerations left my head since the shooting. "But I should pay you back for—"

Sternness. "No."

"It's only right since you—"

"Taking care of you wasn't a loan. It was a privilege."

It's hard to breathe in this rare bookstore, the air crowded with dust and history and emotion. I throw my arms around Liam's waist. It's much like hugging a column made of marble. He doesn't move the way someone might when being hugged. He doesn't hug me back. That's the way he is… it's hard for him to accept affection. Hard for him to bear it. I make him anyway, because my joy can't be contained.

And I think… maybe hugging him more will make him accept it easier.

Slowly his arms come around me. He holds me awkwardly. Sex, he can do. Hugs are still hard for him. He squeezes too soft and too hard. I'll accept this broken hug, but then something happens, something changes, and it feels right. Like our bodies have worked it out. They've communicated in the way that only cells can do. It's biology, this hug.

He looks down at me. His expression is still stern, but there's something in his green eyes I've never seen before. It might be wonder. Maybe even relief.

I purchase the manuscript and arrange for its safe delivery to the chateau. I almost don't need to go next door, but we're already here and I don't want this day to end.

LIAM

THE BOOKSTORE HAS a highbrow history in literature, having been visited by famous writers of literature: Ernest Hemingway, F. Scott Fitzgerald, and Anaïs Nin. There are cots upstairs where transient, upcoming writers have slept with only the promise that they write. A cursory investigation revealed no connection to Samantha, her father, or anything remotely political. It appears to be simply a bookstore with a colorful past.

Then again, sometimes appearances are deceiving.

The woman who may or may not be Samantha's mother held a bag from here. Coincidence? I don't know. Samantha's brown eyes sparkle. She looks high on the excitement of the day. It's the way she looks when she masters a new complex piece.

It isn't in me to tell her no right now. Or maybe ever.

She does own me.

Poetry. Literature. History. We walk through various rooms. The narrow space and crowd keeps a few feet between us. She turns a corner. A moment passes before I turn it, too. There's nothing else for it unless I want to shove people out of the way.

The farther she goes, the more I feel the pull.

Will it always be like this?

A string from the center of my chest to hers. Is this love?

We come full circle to the cash registers. She hasn't collected any books in her arms. A glance back at me. In her eyes I see the tacit agreement to leave the crowded shop. Man and woman cross between us, their expressions almost drowsy with love. Honeymooners. "We have to go upstairs," the woman says to the man. "We have to see the notes."

A question forms in Samantha's eyes. "What notes?" she mouths to me.

Josh submitted a report on the background of

the bookstore after he visited. "Writers who've worked in residence upstairs leave a short autobiographical page about themselves. I assume that's what she means."

Before I finish speaking I know we'll have to go upstairs.

We pass under painted words. *Be not inhospitable to strangers lest they be angels in disguise.* It's a very Samantha-esque sentiment. I suppose if I had a bookstore it would say: be not trusting of strangers, lest they be devils in disguise.

Then again, the doors would probably be locked.

We find a hundred lives transcribed onto blue paper, some of it written by hand, some of it done with the typewriters placed around the small second floor. They're stacked on the desk and tacked to the wall. There doesn't seem to be any order. How would they be found? I have to remind myself these aren't reports filed in a security company. These are... what? Art? Stories? Diary entries? A few messages are interspersed between the notes on display, such as you might find etched into a tree. Or somewhere less savory.

The literary equivalent of a bathroom wall.

One such piece of blue paper has been folded in thirds. On the outside it's written: Ms. S.

Brooks in a neat looping script. We see it at the same time. I feel her freeze. If I had seen it first, then what? Would I have tried to keep it from her? Maybe. At least until I know what's inside. She has it in her hands, ripped open, before I can stop her.

I take a walk in Tuileries on Friday afternoons.

CHAPTER FOURTEEN

People isolated from sound sometimes experience false sensory inputs. In one study, participants were placed in a dark and silent room for 15 minutes. Some test subjects saw objects that were not there, five had hallucinations of faces, four reported a heightened sense of smell, and two felt there was an evil presence in the chamber with them.

SAMANTHA

I'M IN THE sitting room. The violin is on the sofa opposite me. We're engaged in a staring contest. I managed to take it out of the case this morning, so I think I'm winning.

The door opens behind me, but I don't break my concentration. Even though it means someone else will now be witnessing my cowardice. Someone hitches on the back of the sofa I'm on. Too small to be Liam or Josh. They'd probably break the fragile antique if they tried that.

"What are we doing?" Isa says.

"Thinking."

"Oh good," she says. "I thought maybe you were in a staring contest with an inanimate object.

That would be concerning."

"First of all, a violin isn't exactly inanimate. It's very animated when I'm playing it." I sigh at myself. "And second of all, I'm winning the staring contest."

She slides into the seat next to me. "I'll keep you company."

Out of the corner of my eye I see her wide silk skirt in deep emerald. Does she always dress like a queen? "I'm trying to figure out the longest I ever went without playing. Well, once I started. I suppose the longest time was when I was a baby."

"I thought you were one of those genius freaks who could play before you opened your eyes. Isn't that what Fransisco said? You were a child prodigy?"

"I could open my eyes. I could walk and talk."

"So who sets the bar? Who says, this kid is good enough to be a prodigy?"

The music community could be fickle. It could also eat its own. "There's usually disagreement. But then people disagree about the level of talent in adults, too."

"Did anyone dare to say that Samantha Brooks wasn't a prodigy?"

That makes me laugh. "My violin teacher. She hated me, I think. Or she hated the violin. She used to make me put my fingers in these positions that only made sense for bigger hands. Then the music would come out bad. If she just let me play, it would sound perfect."

"Maybe she was jealous."

"I used to sneak into the music room at lunchtime to play. Lucky for me the history teacher heard me playing. She played the piano, but not at a professional level. Still, she knew what she heard. She got the principal involved, and the music teacher had to give me more advanced music after that."

"I bet that pissed her off."

"So much. She started using a ruler on my knuckles if I didn't do it her way. I spent a lot of that year with red lines imprinted on the backs of my hands." It was a weird kind of conditioning. It never bothered me later when my hands would ache or bleed. I learned to play that way. "Then we moved away."

"Ugh. I hope she sees your concert at the Palais Garnier and cries."

"She was old back then. She might be dead now."

"That's inconsiderate of her, being dead before you can get your comeuppance."

"People have a way of coming back from the

dead around me," I mutter, my thoughts turning dark as I stare at the shape of the violin. It's always been a contrast of lines and curves, of soft wood and taut strings. It looks the same as it always did, and somehow foreign, too.

The door opens and closes again. Sunlight spills across the room at a diagonal. It had been a direct shot through the window when I started. The day is passing. No notes have been played.

Bethany sits beside me. "Why are you watching your violin?"

"Staring contest," Isa says from the other side of the sofa.

"Who's winning?"

Isa snorts. "Not Samantha."

Probably accurate. The violin can wait all day. All year. All century. I'm the one who's running out of time. "How long have you gone without dancing?" I ask Bethany.

"Oh, this one time I was on the silks. Someone had misplaced a beam. My ankle shattered. I wasn't even supposed to walk for weeks, much less dance. I almost died." She sounds very earnest, not like someone exaggerating to make a point. And I already know she isn't prone to drama.

"Was it scary to start again?"

"No, I couldn't actually stop. I kept dancing

in my room. I'd tell myself I'd only use my left leg, that I'd be so careful, but I'd always end up re-injuring myself. Romeo actually tied me to the bed so I'd stop making it worse."

"Kinky," Isa says.

I stop glaring at the violin long enough to glance at Bethany. Liam's constant movement, his continual re-injuring of himself, had seemed pointless. Irrational. I'm not so conceited to think everything he does is about me, but using his pain as a way to punish me had been the only explanation that made sense. "You did it even though you knew it would take longer to heal."

She shakes her head, though not in disagreement. More like she's dismayed at herself. "Maybe it's like an addiction. Like crack. We'd beg, borrow, or steal to keep doing it."

An addiction. That does explain the way I felt about my violin.

It also explains why I've been so afraid to start again. I never learned how to play in moderation. Rain or shine. Cold or hot. No matter what, I played and played. The world around me could have fallen apart. The world around me *did* fall apart. Which means that if I start playing again, I'll lose myself. I feel like I've been holding my sanity with my bare hands. What happens when I pick up the violin instead?

CHAPTER FIFTEEN

A test chamber at Orfield Laboratories has 3.3-foot-thick fiberglass acoustic wedges, double walls of insulated steel, and foot-thick concrete. It is 99.99% sound absorbent. The founder challenges people to see how long they can stay in the room. The record is 45 minutes.

LIAM

FRIDAY MORNING THERE'S a knock at the sitting room. I open it, expecting to find Frans. We made plans to scout the Tuileries before I take Samantha there. It's unlikely anyone will prepare to ambush us in such an open space, but I don't want to take the chance.

Alexander Fox. That's who stands at the door.

Technically, Samantha's door. My eyes narrow. "Yes?"

A frown. He doesn't like that I'm answering her door. That's fine, since I don't like that he's knocking on it. "I came to speak to Samantha."

"About what?"

"About the concert."

"I'll see if she's available." I close the door.

The fact that I take pleasure in doing so is completely coincidental. No one has unfettered access to her. Except me.

She's doing the staring thing with her violin again.

I push it aside to sit down in front of her. Her brown eyes focus on me. "Hi."

"Hello. Alexander Fox came to see you."

She looks around the room as if expecting to see him in a chair. I try not to let it bother me, the way she disconnects from the world. It's part of the healing process. Or is it part of the staying-hurt process? It's hard to tell the difference sometimes.

"What did he want?"

"To talk to you about the concert."

She sighs. "He wants to know what I'm going to play."

"Tell him to wait."

"These things are usually decided way in advance. That way the orchestra can prepare. As it is Romeo and Bethany have had to make arrangements without me."

"Tell him to wait."

Another glance around the room. "Well, I can try. Assuming he comes back."

"I think he's at the door."

A wide-eyed look. "Right now?"

"Probably."

"Why didn't you say that?"

"This way he has practice waiting."

An exasperated sigh. She mutters something about men, which is probably generous. I can only imagine if she knew what thoughts went through my head. He conspired to take her away from me. He offered to hide her from me. The fact that he thought he protected her is the only thing that keeps me from throwing a punch.

SAMANTHA

I EXPECT THE Tuileries Gardens to have more flowers. Or bushes. Trees?

There's a lot of stone walkways. And grass. Large expanses of grass. The whole gardens are bigger than I would have expected, too. Enough that it's not immediately clear how we would meet someone.

Naturally, Liam didn't want me to come.

Except he couldn't count on anyone showing up if they didn't see me in the park. And I wasn't going to miss the chance to meet the mother who left me. I'm not thinking there'll be a sweet reunion. When your mother leaves you to fate and a barren Russian orphanage, there aren't a lot of nice feelings left. She asked for this meeting, arranged it, and I want to find out what she has to say. It could be the information we're in Paris to uncover.

We walk for fifteen minutes. Or an hour. It's hard to tell because I'm breathing hard, my muscles taut. I'm braced for an altercation. A fight or flight. Liam pulls me down to sit at a bench while he murmurs into his watch. "East side entrance," comes the response.

I turn to the east in time to see an older woman turn down the path toward us. Liam starts to rise, to place his body between mine and hers. I put my hand on his arm. "Let me."

"Samantha."

"You can't protect me forever. Let me go."

I didn't mean it to be so poignant, but he looks at me as if I'm asking for him to say goodbye. Those green eyes, so familiar and yet always a surprise. So vibrant for someone who never shows emotion. Except for now, when he looks half-broken.

"Go," he says, his voice hoarse.

I didn't mean it like that. The words hover on my tongue. I'm not sure they're true, though. Eventually he'll have to let me go. It might as well be now, when I'm in a foreign land, with family I can't even recognize on sight, unable to play the instrument that's been like a limb to me. A complete loss. A hard separation from the Samantha from before and after.

The woman stops when she sees me walking towards her.

Wrinkles frame her eyes and mouth. Laugh lines. Frown lines. A lifetime lived without me in it. The brown eyes, though. Those are familiar. They look back at me in the mirror. "Hello," I say, which feels inane to say to a long-lost mother.

It also feels like more than she deserves.

"You look beautiful," she says, with those mine/not-mine eyes.

"Why did you find me?" Of course I wouldn't have asked this question if she had shown up at the orphanage. Or even years later, on Liam's doorstep. I think even if she'd found me on the US leg of the tour, I would have embraced her. Hopeful and hopeless.

"Take a walk with me."

An order from a parent who does not have the right to give it.

I look back at the man who does have my respect—not quite a parent. Not quite a lover. He waits with his hands behind his back in a strict military bearing. I suppose that's who's in the gardens with me today. The soldier.

With a nod I fall into step beside her. She has an uneven gait, her left leg strained from some old injury. It's cruel, I think, that I have the urge to ask her about it. That I have the urge to offer my arm to ease her way. Cruel, when she couldn't spare a minute for me.

She sighs. "Maybe it was too much to hope you'd be happy."

Maybe it was too much to hope you'd be a mother. There's more bitterness in the thought than I expected. I don't sit with this grief every day. There's a mother-shaped hole inside me, grown over with moss and ivy. It doesn't have to be seen, but when I pull away the vegetation of everyday life, there it is. "Yes."

"Do you remember me?"

There are impressions of soft skin and hard curls, the smell of jasmine and hairspray. I remember the colorful batik fabric she wore, though she's in more modern, plain clothing now. "Not very much. Do you remember me?"

A small laugh. "More than I would like, sometimes."

I'm determined not to feel bad for her, but a little sympathy seeps in. The curse of being human, to feel empathy for someone else, even if they don't feel any for you. "The man back there, he's the only parent I've really known."

She nods her head, as if absorbing a blow, accepting it. "He's more than a parent."

"How do you know?"

"I went to your shows in the US. Almost all of them."

There's a crack in my heart, but it's not going to let her in. It's only going to fracture. Any orphan wants to have parents. Any orphan dreams of it. I wasn't different that way, except that I thought she was dead. "Why did Daddy say you died?"

"Maybe he thought it would be easier for you to handle that way."

"It wasn't."

"More likely he did it to protect me. If I were dead, then no one could come after me to use against him. No one could threaten me to get what they wanted from him."

The words raise alarm along my spine. If someone could threaten her to get to him, they could threaten me. Is that what happened? No, he turned the gun on me in Carnegie Hall.

That's something a daughter doesn't forget.

"Your father did bad things. I think at the

beginning he did it for the right reasons."

"There are no right reasons for treason."

That earns me a sharp glance.

Is that how I look when I'm displeased with Liam? God, how strange to see my face on someone else. Even stranger because it's so ordinary. It's something everyone with a family would know. Not rare. Not heartbreaking.

"He thought he was doing something important. Or maybe he only wanted to believe that. Then it became about the money. Then… it was too late to leave, even if he wanted to. Well, he probably didn't want to. He liked the money too much."

"Is that why you left him?"

"I left him because I was afraid. I was afraid of the men he was in business with, the people, the entire countries who felt they owned him because of what they paid."

"The songs he taught me—"

"He called it his insurance policy."

Greed and ambition. The most common human motivations. I glance back at Liam, who has never been moved by either one of those things. We stop at a small gathering of flowers, a rare spot of color in a landscape of white concrete and green grass. A red ladybug rests on a wide green leaf. It means good luck, Bethany said. This particular ladybug must not have gotten the message.

"Insurance how?"

"It was a back door. A code that could get into the system. Even having it would prove that corruption had happened. That he could also influence the results meant he was a force to be reckoned with."

"I don't understand. What system?"

"Oh. You didn't know? The electronic voting system."

Dear God. There is no excuse for treason, but this is somehow more than I expected. I thought there would be secrets handed over. Maybe information about weaponry. The kind that wouldn't actually get used because we weren't at war.

This has very real, very scary consequences.

"I've already written down the musical score in detail." A broken laugh escapes me. "I played most of it for hundreds of people before the shots rang out. It's recorded. Why are they still after me if this back door is already out there?"

"Because you are the only link to your father and them. You are the link that will be used to assassinate them privately or declare war publicly. You are the most dangerous person in the world to some of the most dangerous people."

CHAPTER SIXTEEN

Emperor Napoleon III launched an architectural design competition for the design of the new opera house. Charles Garnier's project was one of about 170 submitted.

SAMANTHA

PEOPLE EITHER LOVE or hate the Palais Garnier.

It has its own style, which is really a nice way of saying it borrows from many other styles, taking only the most loud and ostentatious parts. Seventy-three sculptors created the outside cornices and embellishments alone.

A less sympathetic observer might call it garish.

As a child it had been overwhelming.

Now that I stand before the grand staircase that splits to either side of the theater, I can't help but feel awe. How could I not? It's a monument to art. Recognition of music's place in society's consciousness. The elaborate showmanship of the shows in the US aren't necessary here. The setting provides the grandeur.

We only need to add music.

Easier said than done. Liam appears behind the central stairs. He's been liaising with the house security for days now. His footsteps echo off marble, bronze, and canvas paintings on the ceiling. His expression looks as severe as a statue. "Are you ready?"

"Are you afraid I'm going to stand up there and not play a note?"

He's distracted by the logistics of safety. The entrances, the exits. The armed guards. It's reflected in the lightness of his green eyes. Slowly he focuses on me. He doesn't look worried about what I said though. "Of course not."

"There's no *of course not.* I haven't played in months."

"Some things you don't forget how to do, no matter how long it's been."

We're clearly talking about the violin. Or maybe about physical agility, the way that Bethany described. We're definitely not talking about sex, but my cheeks heat as if he's said something dirty. It feels even more taboo that we're talking about it here, at the premiere theater in the world, in a place meant to be packed with people.

My face feels warm. "It won't be good to be rusty, either."

He looks amused. He must know what I'm thinking about. "You won't be rusty. But even if you were, you'd still play better than anyone else."

"You sound like a proud—"

His gaze sharpens. "I sound like a proud father?"

It comes out as a whisper. "Yes."

"I'll never be able to separate that part of me. The man who made you breakfast before school and signed your permission slips. The man who knew you would conquer the world. I'll never be able to stop wanting to protect you, Samantha."

And I would never stop being the grateful orphan taken in by him.

Where does that leave us?

He takes my hand and leads me up the stairs to the Grand Foyer. Paintings cover the sixty-foot ceilings, each framed with elaborate gilt. It's not hard to see the dismay through the eyes of the common citizen. What is the usefulness of luxury to a person who can't buy bread? The French underwent a particularly bloody revolution in response to this sort of excess. Is it irresponsible? Or full of hope? What a strange dichotomy to walk.

We come to the theater. A gasp escapes me.

Elaborate carvings line the balcony. Red velvet covers the seats. The chandelier rises high and proud, uncaring about whether a poor man needs to eat. It's beautiful and troubling, a mixture I find more common the older I get. Everything felt so black and white when I was young. Playing the violin well was a good thing. Having parents who were alive was a good thing. Now I have both, but the only thing I want stands beside me.

"The theater was the inspiration for Phantom of the Opera."

"I visited the canals this morning."

The canals, which are beneath us right now. We're standing on top of the Phantom's supposed lair. All I know is what I've seen in the movie version. "Does it look like an underground Venice?"

"It looks like a sewer."

Disappointment sinks in my stomach. "That's less romantic."

"If it makes you feel better, the chandelier actually fell during a performance."

Even in the daytime, with the lights off, a thousand crystals shimmer. "Because the Phantom was angry that Christine didn't get the lead role?" I ask hopefully.

"More likely because seven tons of bronze weren't properly counterbalanced."

"You're determined to ruin my fun."

A slight smile. "It gets worse. I want to show you the emergency exits. I'm going to be backstage with you, but in case anything happens I want you to be able to get yourself to safety."

"In case anything happens. You mean in case you get shot."

He doesn't answer. He's a bronze statue that stands at the corner of the building, a sentry, a gargoyle with a handsome jaw. There is nothing that reaches through the metal exterior. "You don't wait for me. You don't take me with you. You—"

"If you get shot I don't think you'll get to tell me what to do."

The exterior cracks, revealing a man at the edge of his limits. He drags me into the shadows. His mouth slams on mine, and I think he's going to kiss me—but he doesn't. Instead he breathes in deep. It's half kiss, half breath as our bodies find the same rhythm.

"I need to stop them once and for all. The only way I can do that is if I know you're safe. Understand? Promise me you'll leave me behind. Promise me you'll stay safe. If I'm worried about you, I'm already dead."

A shudder down the length of my body. It doesn't matter that warm air barely circulates in the daytime. Doesn't matter that we're safe at this moment. A chill seeps out from his words. It encompasses my arms, my chest, my heart. He gives me a little shake, not enough to hurt. Enough to demand. "I promise," I say, gasping out the word. It's forced from me, this promise. It's the only thing I can do in the face of his desperate demand.

LIAM

WE RAN BACKGROUND checks on the members of the orchestra, on the stagehands. We even ran cursory checks on the names on the tickets, but it would be too easy to fake ID for the purchase. Despite strong objections from the company managing the performance, metal detectors and X-ray conveyers block the entrances. Our methods rival any embassy. Any airport. On the surface we're completely safe. My gut has kept me alive this long. It tells me that something is going to happen tonight.

Dread. Relief. If they didn't strike tonight we'd have to keep putting her on stages, using her as bait. Or worry that they'd try to get at her in the chateau. I want them to reveal themselves when I have armed men under my command sitting in every section.

I want them with bullets in their brains, but I'll have to settle for taking them alive. If we have that, if we can pull a confession out of them, if we can prove the link without Samantha, then she won't pose a threat to them anymore.

That's the only way she'll be free.

Women mill around in designer eveningwear and glittering heels. Men laugh the too-loud chuckle they do in the company of other powerful men. The crowd consumes enough champagne to fill the caverns downstairs.

I run the check-ins to each man stationed in the foyer, the auditorium, and outside. They come back like clockwork. It doesn't reassure me. If anything, the tension tightens in my body.

I study the faces of each patron, wondering which one hides behind a mask of careless high society. I knew that Ambassador Brooks was involved in dirty business, but what Samantha's mother revealed proves this goes much, much higher than him. Those are the kind of people with the resources to get into an embassy or an airport undetected.

The kind of people who commit treason and walk away unscathed.

Not tonight.

Lights above us blink three times. It's time for the show.

There are additional credentials required to go backstage. I swipe my pass. No one gets special treatment tonight. Not Josh. Not me. Bethany and Romeo are doing stretches in the corner. Dissonant sounds come from the stage, where an orchestra waits behind the canvas curtain. I know the background of every stagehand who hurries around, pulling ropes and messing with the lights. I know who owes money and whose daddy went to prison.

Samantha crouches beside her violin case as if she's giving it a pep talk.

Are you afraid I'm going to stand up there and not play a note?

I'm not sure if she's worried about it, but I'm not. The fact that she hasn't played since the violin went back in her possession? That's pure stubbornness. My fault, for trying to command her into doing it. The old Samantha would have jumped to obey me. The new Samantha takes pleasure in independence. More than that, she likes giving commands to me. I'm just perverse enough to enjoy that, too.

I kneel beside her, flicking open the locks on the case. "If you get nervous, don't picture the crowd naked."

Her hands press together. Like a prayer. "No?"

"Picture me naked."

A breathless laugh. "I don't think that will make me less nervous."

"No?" I ask, using the same European lilt she used.

"You're kind of intimidating when you're naked. Did you know that soldiers fighting the Romans used to fight naked? They would hold their weapons. That's it."

"That sounds impractical."

"Because they're not wearing armor?"

"That. And because of the places mud will end up."

She laughs before sobering. "I'm going to play the song I wrote. I think that's part of the problem. It was interrupted. It was unfinished. And I think... it doesn't matter that my father gave me part of it. I mean, it does matter. It's not only that melody. It's not only the backdoor code. It's the song I built on top of that."

The song she built on top of what her father

gave her. A metaphor for her strength. Her ability to build a palace from the rubble of her childhood. *I haven't played in months.* As if that could stop her. Nothing can. Not even fear. I didn't need to demand that she play. She would do it when she's ready. Tonight. Now. Lights dim. The curtain rises.

She picks up the violin and bow.

CHAPTER SEVENTEEN

Composer Claude Debussy wrote the now famous Clair de Lune early in his career. He didn't want to publish it because it wasn't in his mature style, but eventually, fifteen years later, he accepted an offer from a publisher.

SAMANTHA

I'M WEARING A black satin dress from an up-and-coming designer in Paris. Like most of the arts, music has a decided bias towards old, white men. So does fashion. That's why I was grateful to find a woman about my age with only education—and an original perspective—to recommend her. Plus, she put pockets in my dress. Pockets in my couture dress!

That's where I put the music sheet from Debussy.

In the bookstore it had seemed almost too holy to touch, this paper. There's still a sense of unreality about it. The history alone—that someone wrote this a hundred years ago. The more I hold it, though, the more I feel the man behind the legacy. His uncertainty and his hope. His musical genius shaded into the notes.

Of course, he was one of those old, white men who saw opportunities that women of color never saw during his time. Women of color like me. A hundred years later, I'm standing on the stage where he performed. Did he have the same worry about what critics would say? Did he worry that he would stand in front of a crowd and forget how to play?

Did he feel the same unexpected serenity, as if every afternoon of practice, every night of dreaming, every second of yearning, led to this moment?

There is no dramatic entry from the back of the audience, no characters in costume, no tethers hanging from the ceiling. It's a traditional format befitting a traditional venue. Bethany and Romeo complete an excerpt from La Bayadere to much applause.

When my turn arrives, there is not even an announcement. They will know who it is by the order in the program. Or by recognizing the hand that plays. That's the way it's done.

A hush covers the audience.

With my violin in one hand and bow in the other, I walk to the front of the stage. A thunderous applause shakes the timbers beneath my feet. Years ago I might have felt undeserving. Their clear anticipation might have even made me more nervous—after all, it will be that much worse if I disappoint them.

Now I close my eyes and let the energy wash over me.

There's something very special about performing. It's more than the accolades or even the chance to share my music. There's a communion.

A community established in the space of twenty minutes.

The auditorium quiets.

I turn to see Liam waiting in the wings. He doesn't watch me. Instead his eyes are on the seats in front of me. He's ready to throw himself in front of me again. Ready to die so that I can play my music. If that doesn't inspire me to greatness, I don't know what would. Whatever similarities I may share with Claude Debussy, I don't think he was worried about someone shooting him during a performance to cover up a political conspiracy.

A microphone stands in front of the stage in case I wish to speak. The program doesn't say what I'm going to play, considering I didn't know until last night. A courier hand-delivered the sheet music to the pianist this morning.

I lean close enough to feel the static on my lips. "Brooks Sonata Number One."

The applause deafens me.

They know they're hearing something for the first time.

I lift the violin. The bow tilts. And I play.

LIAM

ALL MY ATTENTION belongs on the audience.

The music filters into my consciousness, breaking through years of training, a lifetime of deprivation. Enough to know that she changed the composition. The refrain from her father still sits inside it. It plays like a haunting melody. A memory.

The sonata rises and falls, rises and falls. The crowd looks spellbound.

I'm back in the seaside flat, in a place of both peace and yearning. Her music puts me there. It makes me long for something that would only disappoint me in reality. It makes me dream of the impossible. It's everything she's ever been to me.

When the last note plays, there's a beat of heartbreak. It's over.

Then the room erupts into a standing ovation.

It isn't time for this. Applause, yes. A standing ovation, no. They give her one anyway. I fight every muscle in my body to keep from running onto the stage. She deserves this. No one pulls a gun. No one takes a shot. Not even when she walks back offstage, passing by the soprano who will sing before intermission.

Samantha launches herself into my arms, and I catch her, spinning us both around until we're half-hidden from even the backstage crew.

"I did it," she whispers, mindful of the performance.

Her eyes glitter with wonder. It's too much for a man to resist.

I taste her excitement, her glory in this moment. She kisses me back with a passion much like her sonata, a rise and a fall, a rise and a fall, until I'm spellbound like two thousand other people in the theater. "I love you," I murmur against her lips. Once I start I can't stop. "I want you. I need you. Marry me. Whatever you want I'll give to you."

Her breath catches, and then she's kissing me back. The eroticism of her tongue entrances me, making me imagine us alone. I want to keep this dress on her, if only so I can see how adorable she looks when she shows me it has pockets. I hold her body tight against mine, and it's almost, *almost* enough. I pull back. "Is that a yes?"

The soprano reaches a pinnacle, and the sweet song moves between us, around us, wrapping us in a cocoon no one else can reach. "Yes," she whispers.

She plays twice more the second half of the show. Twice more, when I know she's going to marry me. It's enough to make a man glad for those nights in the well, if it led to this. Nothing happens. No weapons found on entry. No discrepancies with the tickets. There is no disturbance in the audience, and I think we might escape with the perfect night.

As the headliner she plays the final piece. She plays the Claude Debussy piece that she carries in her dress. It remains folded out of sight, because she knows it by heart. And because it only contains the first refrains anyway. Her notes ring out clear and true.

The applause threatens to bring down the Palais Garnier.

After an encore she skips toward me, and I catch her in a circle. My God. She makes me feel hopeful, when I wouldn't have thought I knew the meaning. Like a child before ever seeing the bottom of the well. Before the beatings. Before the hunger pains.

She makes me feel like a new person.

"Did anything happen?" she asks.

"You agreed to marry me," I say, teasing. Liam North. I actually teased the woman I love. That happened. The world is very strange sometimes. She grins up at me. Then Bethany and Romeo are there, and she's hugging them, exclaiming over their performances.

I turn away to do the security check into my watch. "Report. Webb."

"Clear."

"Rogers."

"Clear."

"North."

Silence.

My heartbeat slows. My eyesight sharpens. The body prepares itself for battle even while the mind rebels at the idea. "North." Nothing. "Joshua," I say, breaking protocol. No response. Dread forms in my stomach, but I push it aside. This is war.

Samantha stands like a queen, her black dress billowing. The other performers have disappeared into the milling stage performers. With the curtain down, backstage is chaos. A heavy saturation of sound comes from the audience as people leave their seats.

"What's wrong?"

It doesn't occur to me to lie. "It's Josh."

Her eyes turn round. "He's hurt?"

Probably. If he's not answering, he's probably dead. My mind makes the calculations even though I can't—No. Not my brother. "Rogers," I say into my watch. He's the closest one in position. "Confirm North's status."

"I'm fine here. Your brother needs you. Go."

"I can't leave you."

"I'm not going to be responsible for his death." She reaches up to cup my cheek. "And I'm not going to let you feel that guilt. Help him."

Love is a bastard. It doesn't fight fair. "Samantha."

"I know the exits. I know the protocol. I'll be safe when you get back."

There's a crackle over the radio. My brother needs me, and damn it, I need him. I press a hard, uncompromising kiss to Samantha's lips before I open a door in the stage and help her step down. It leads to the cavern, where Webb is stationed. I take off at a sprint.

Even though it may already be too late.

CHAPTER EIGHTEEN

Fire fighters in Paris do underwater training beneath the Palais Garnier. The brigade's motto is sauver ou périr, *which means* save or perish.

JOSH

EVERY MISSION IS a suicide mission when you don't care about dying.

That's what my brother never understood. He's always wanted to live. Bethany knows. I think it's why she keeps her distance from me. She may not know precisely why, but she senses the darkness inside me. Smart girl.

The night was too quiet. The men under our command started the night full of tension. With every passing song, with every round of applause, the alertness left them—like air being let out of a balloon. They still waited at their post, but they didn't expect violence.

I always expect violence. That's why I'm good at my job.

The concert ends. There is zero air in the

fucking balloon. That's when light flashes on the roof of the pharmacy across the street. It's not an electronic kind of light. Not a phone or a flashlight. It looks like a mirror reflecting the moon. That's some old-school KGB shit, like Morse code or invisible ink. I calculate the angle it would take for someone to see it and round the corner—in time to see a man wearing black drop from the building.

I pull my weapon, but he gets a shot off first—with the dull sound that accompanies a silencer. Pain blasts through my arm. *Motherfucker*. I chase him around the corner, wondering how many bastards he brought with him.

The back of my mind works through the strategy. How did he get onto the roof in the first place? We've had this building locked down for a week. Unless he's been up there before then. Hiding in one of the many crevices. Pissing into a water bottle. Jesus.

He sprints around a corner, and I follow him. Dead end.

A wild glance behind him.

I straighten. "Gotcha."

He raises his pistol. I pull mine, but he's not pointing it at me. He shoots himself in the head. No capture. I bend down to check him for ID.

Nothing. Every mission is a suicide mission if you aren't afraid to die. I pick up his weapon. It's Russian made. I bet the serial number has been filed off. A search of his pockets reveals a radio. We can use this to find the others. As long as we get someone alive, we can turn them over to the State Department and lift the threat to Samantha. I raise my hand to speak into my watch.

A burst of pain at the back of my skull.

The world goes dark.

SAMANTHA

THE CAVERNS LOOK like a sewer. Unfortunately, Liam was right about that. They don't smell amazing, either. The only good news is that there's a walkway out of the water. I climb down a metal ladder and wait at the bottom, worrying over Josh. He's kind of an asshole, but I still love him like an uncle. Or a brother, I suppose, if I'm really going to marry Liam.

I love you. I want you. I need you. Marry me. Whatever you want I'll give to you.

There's no time to feel joy over his proposal. It sparks in my chest anyway, inappropriate in this moment of danger. What could have happened to Josh? I want to hope for a communication malfunction. Or maybe confusion over the procedure. I hope he's going to be found in a stairwell with a French countess, shirking his duties so he can have sex. Anything would be better than finding out he's hurt.

Voices echo off the stone around me. My blood turns to ice.

Water laps softly against the edge. More voices. I'm not alone down here.

It's not Liam. I can tell from the timbre of the voice. And the fact that he isn't calling my name. It's too soon for him to be back, which means these are the people after me. There is a natural sense of self-preservation. I don't want to die in this cavern, even if there is a poetic symmetry to doing it where Christine was captured by the Phantom. More than that, I don't want Liam to live with the guilt. He'd never forgive himself.

I look around for a place to hide. There's only stone down here. And water.

I press along the wall, scooting back, back, back. My foot slips into a puddle. The splash makes my heart stop. The voices continue, the rhythm unbroken. They didn't hear. Or they assumed it was a drop from the ceiling into the never-ending caverns.

My foot slips again, this time almost toppling

me. I glance back to see the faintest, far-away ripples. It looks like some kind of hole. A well. I'll be disguised down there. Even now I can barely see any glint of light on the water's surface.

I turn to kneel at the edge and hang from my hands.

Then I let go.

CHAPTER NINETEEN

After two decades of experimental forms, Debussy finally decided to write in the ultra-traditional form for his first and only violin sonata. Its debut was his last public performance before his death.

LIAM

A BLACK FORM sprawls in the alley. Dark liquid reflects the moonlight. The carnage of a gunshot to the jaw. My stomach clenches. There isn't any gore that could make me heave, but the thought of my brother threatens my calm.

Calm is everything to a soldier.

I touch two fingers to his temple to turn him. As soon as I do, I know it's not Josh. The wrong shape, the wrong hair color. Relief almost steals my voice. "Unidentified white male," I say into my watch. "DOA. Keep looking."

That night he held Elijah up above the water, I swore I'd never put them in danger again. They followed me into the military because it was the only thing we knew how to do. It wasn't even the violence that drew us. It was the act of survival. What was life without the constant threat of death? I didn't want them to join North Security. I tried to keep them out of combat. It didn't always work, but none of that mattered when it came to protecting Samantha.

Samantha. She's back in the theater, and any hope that this was a false alarm has been shattered with the discovery of the dead body. Do I head back to the caverns? Or do I find my brother? I'm torn between the woman I love and the man that's flesh and blood.

I'm not going to let you feel that guilt. Help him.

He might be lying in a pool of blood like this sorry bastard.

"Boss," comes a voice that I recognize as Webb. "We found something on the roof. One of these angel sculptures up here? It had a false side. There's enough meal packs in here to last a month. And it smells rank."

That explains how they got past our defenses. They were already here.

Be not inhospitable to strangers lest they be angels in disguise.

What if the angels are strangers in disguise?

"Code Omega," I say, and in case there's any doubt: "Shut the place down."

We had a hundred different scenarios. Ten different responses. This one's the most extreme. The kitchen sink. The French police are going to shit their pants over what happens next, but with my brother and my future wife in danger, I don't care.

There is a small part of my brain that worries for Samantha when the flashbangs drop into the caverns. I need her to be strong for this. What's more important is that anyone with her is immobilized. A moan draws my attention farther back in the alley.

I draw my weapon and stride over.

Josh stares down the barrel of my gun. "Hell," he says.

His eyes are dilated. I check him for gunshot wounds. He mumbles something that I can't understand. It might be "Bethany." Without ceremony I sling him over my shoulders in a fireman's carry. I make it back in time to hear the sirens wail. Webb guards the entrance to the caverns. I shove Josh at him, who curses me in three different languages.

I didn't even know he spoke Arabic.

Then I'm climbing down the metal stairs, fighting the panic.

"Samantha!"

Fear.

Real fear, the kind that puts metal in my mouth. I'm not sure I've felt this since I was trapped at the bottom of the well. I've fought long and hard so I'd never have to feel fear again, but loving Samantha's made me vulnerable. It's made me weak.

Liam. It's more the suggestions of sound than actual vibration. The cave walls seem to echo it back, mocking me, making me wonder if it's just hopefulness. Webb. And, Christ, so is Josh. He's probably going to fall into the water.

Frans climbs down after them, looking out of place in his bespoke tux, except I know that he can handle himself in combat. "I found Rogers. He's got three of them on the floor face down. Alive. One of them's already talking. The other two can't shut him up."

That should be a relief. That's what we need to end the threat to Samantha, except that she's not here. She's not in my arms. What if she's already hurt? It was my own goddamn hubris to think I could save them both—my brother and my lover. An impossible choice.

"Samantha! Say something. Let me hear you."

"Liam!"

This time I'm sure she answered me, but the

call bounces off the walls, making the source unclear. "Split up," I say without waiting to see if they obey.

I take the forward path, the darkest one.

"Liam!" She sounds louder now. "I'm down here."

A hard knot in my stomach. I take a step forward. My eyes stare into blackness. Then she turns her face toward me, pale and so small. She's in a well. That's all I can think about. The stench of old water. The creatures that live in the bottom of the earth. It was something I knew well. I would have killed so that Samantha never knew that. I would have died for it.

"A rope." My voice comes out hoarse. I turn to call back louder. "I found her. We need rope. Get some goddamn rope. Now."

SAMANTHA

PANIC CLAWS AT the edges of my mind.

The darkness tries to close in, but there is one thought that holds me steady: Liam will find me. When he does, I want to be calm for him. I want to be strong for him. Despite my intentions, I almost sob with relief when I hear him call my name.

A rope is lowered down, and I hook it under my arms. Then I hold on with both my hands, kicking off the side of the cavern so I don't slam into it. When I reach the top, Liam crushes me in a hold that would probably be painful if I weren't numb.

His hands work at my clothes, which have frozen stiff against my skin. On the train he had the presence of mind to drag me into the lavatories. Now he doesn't have that. It's more important that he gets the gown off me, the cold and wet of it. There's probably a hundred diseases in this cloth that he rips from me. The cavern air doesn't even feel cold. It occurs to me belatedly that it's a bad thing, not being able to feel.

There are other men with him. I recognize some of them. Normally Liam would protect my modesty at all costs. Now my safety is more important. My health. He strips me down, not concerned with whether or not they see me. Or maybe too overwrought to notice.

They turn to give me privacy, one by one. To give Liam privacy as he touches my body, every place, not a sensual caress, but making sure it's still there—pulse beating beneath my blueish skin. Josh turns away first. Then Frans. Then Romeo. Even Alexander. They form a circle around us, of protection. Of privacy. Liam tears the T-shirt over his head and covers me, finally, so that I have his body warmth. Someone hands back a blanket, thick and hard and pilling, which Liam wraps around me before lifting me into his arms. That's the way we leave the chamber, with him shirtless and me clad in a blanket. Christine was carried down into this place by the Phantom and rescued by her vicomte. I was carried in and taken away by the same person, my villain and my hero, the man who will always be by my side.

CHAPTER TWENTY

In playing Christine's father in this movie, Ramin Karimloo became the only actor to have played all three of Christine's loves. Her father in the movie version, and both Raoul and the Phantom on the stage.

SAMANTHA

EVENING DRAPES SHADOWS across the furniture, across the rugs. It limns Liam's body in a vibrant yellow. Even half-dark, he has never looked so alive to me. Like the soldiers who fought the Romans, he's naked. Impractical, he said. He doesn't wear any armor.

My gaze lingers on his broad shoulders. The strong arms that pulled me out of a cistern. The abs bunched tight from the casual way he sits. There's only a pink line where his scar used to be, almost fully healed now. Muscle forms long lines across his legs, not obscured by the coarse hair across them. In this position there's only a hint of the paler skin of his ass. Only a suggestion of the part between his legs.

He turns to notice me, and I'm struck anew at the deep green of his eyes. Like a gemstone. A vibrant meadow. A thousand things in nature, but he's both the most unique and the most ordinary of them—a man. "I should put you in bed."

"You did that." It had been the only way he relinquished me. Not during the ride in the armored SUV to the chateau or up the stairs. Only in the plush, overlarge bed would he finally set me down. Dirty. Wet. I ruined the sheets. He didn't care.

A doctor arrived to examine me. There are antibiotics and pain medications on the dresser— more a precaution than because I need them. More because Liam demanded the doctor do something. A healthy body can survive a lot.

After all, look at Liam. He spent nights in a place like that as a child. I understand better the isolation that haunts him. The silence becomes almost a physical being, both a companion and a barrier to the rest of the world. This after only thirty minutes in the water. What would happen if a boy were kept there over days, weeks, years?

He allowed me to take a long, warm bath without him only if Isa remained in the bathroom with me, in case I should suddenly lose consciousness or become sick. That had been surprisingly useful. Isa gave me some ideas about what I could do to ease Liam's worry.

Or at least distract him.

The red silk robe I'm wearing belongs to her. It falls only to the middle of my thighs. A silk length cinches it closed at the waist, but there's plenty to see above that, where the sides lean open. Liam tries not to look. Bless him, he tries.

"You're the most noble man I've ever met," I say, tugging at the loose ends.

That earns me a low growl. "You're tired."

The silk flows like liquid off my shoulders. I'm wearing a lacy black bra and matching panties, also courtesy of Isa. It seemed a little pointless to put on underwear with the plan to remove it right away, but she was sure it would help. Now that I saw the muscle clenching in Liam's jaw, I know she's right.

"Not that tired."

"It's the adrenaline. You'll crash soon."

I reach behind me to unhook the bra. It falls forward in my arms, the cups rasping against my nipples. A shiver runs through me. The garment falls to the floor. "Crash with me."

He's not unaffected. The proof of that rises between his legs, no longer at rest but thick and proud. There's no embarrassment about his erection, about his body. He's the picture of masculine arousal. "Don't tempt me, Samantha."

It's all I've wanted to do, tempt him. I realized that down in the water. Before that I wanted him to love me. Not only as a guardian. There were these rules transcribed in my heart. It doesn't matter that they came from the wistfulness of being orphaned. They weren't fair to him. Instead of wanting his love, I'm going to love him. Simple and complex. Immediate and eternal. There's no requirement that he loves me back. *Love is a word. It's a weakness. I protect you. That's all that matters.* Yes, protection would be enough from this man. Maybe one day he would wake up in an ordinary, domestic life and finally believe I won't ever leave. Or maybe he'll doubt me for the rest of his life. I'll make no demands. That's the surest sign of faith I know how to give him.

I hook my thumbs into my panties and push them down my legs. A step out of them. It feels like walking out of an ocean. I'm on the shore now, my toes in the sand. He stares at me like I'm an otherworld creature. *Love isn't a weakness, Liam. Look at me. I'm strong because of you. And I can protect you, too.*

I sink to my knees, but he grasps my wrist.

"No," he says.

"No?"

He turns me so that I'm sitting on the ledge, the waning sun warm on my back, my legs pushed apart by the height of my perch. A palm on my thighs opens me farther. His gaze turns to malachite as he stares at my center. "My turn."

A caveman could not sound more primitive. More possessive.

"Your turn to do what?" I ask, even as he kneels in front of me. My sex clenches in anticipation of his touch. His mouth. *My turn,* as if it's something he's been wanting. "Oh."

His thumb slicks through my core, and I squirm, pressing my back against the window. If anyone takes a walk on the lawn, they'll see my bare bottom. My naked back. My hair falling around my shoulders. If anyone sees me they'll know my legs are spread for him.

LIAM

"SUCH A BRAVE girl," I murmur, my mouth already watering. She smells like saltwater and sunshine. I press my face against her sex, wanting her more than air. A turn to the side. I bite down on the inside of her thigh. The high-pitched sound she makes in response almost has me coming on the carpet like a goddamn teenager.

Her sex glistens with arousal. I slide my tongue to taste her. *Yes.* It's the reassurance I needed. The reassurance I would never have demanded—that she's safe and alive and *here with me.* The terror of the cisterns still nips at my composure. I'm still not convinced she's unscathed. Those kind of experiences can haunt a person. I should know. There was no way to refuse her offering, not with her breasts high and tight, the dark hair between her legs already fragrant. A flick of my tongue on her clit makes her moan.

It's almost enough to distract me from my purpose. Another lick. Another. I could make her come, hear her screams, do it again. I'd be inside her pulsing sex before she could ask, pumping deep enough that she'd forget about earlier, that she'd forget everything.

I clamp down on my urges. *Patience, you bastard.*

Of all people, Samantha deserves my patience. She's certainly waited long enough for this. My dress pants are draped over the chair. I grab them and pull out the black velvet box. "My turn to taste you, yes. I'm going to. It's also my turn to tell you that I love you. That I want you any way that you'll have me—but I hope you'll have me as your husband."

She stares at the black box, looking almost… frightened?

I become aware that I'm naked. She's naked. Maybe she would rather be dressed for a proposal. Maybe she wanted something in the middle of a ballroom of people. Shaking hands take the box from me. She opens it. Tears shield her reaction.

"If you want a regular diamond, we can do that. This was a private sale, and Frans seemed sure… now that I think about it, I have no idea why I would have listened to him."

"It's perfect," she whispers.

"I suppose it's because he's married. That makes you think he knows how it's done. Of course I have no idea how it's done. I'm going to make a million mistakes, but I'll do it with love. With adoration. With gratitude, if you'll let me try."

Her gaze meets mine, swimming with a sense of uncertainty. "I didn't expect this from you. You didn't have to, you know that right? This kind of openness…"

My chest tightens. How could she doubt me? Because I gave her every reason to doubt me. "It was never a question of loving you, Samantha. I always did that. In the right ways. In the wrong ways. In the dirty ways." It's probably unfair that I stroke my thumb along the inside of her thigh as I speak. If it convinces her to stay with me, all the better. Her breath catches. "The only question was whether I could stop trying to sacrifice myself for you."

A tremulous smile. "And can you?"

"You don't want a martyr. God knows you don't need one. I figured that out in the alley outside the Palais Garnier, looking down at a dead body and thinking it might be my brother. There's no honor in giving you up. Both of us lose that way. I was afraid, plain and simple. Afraid you'd leave me. Afraid you *wouldn't* leave me, and you'd see what's underneath this military training. You deserve someone as brave as you. I've decided that's going to be me."

She throws her arms around my neck. I let her tumble us back onto the rug. The black velvet box rolls to a stop beside us. I pull out the ring. It's a two-carat green emerald that once belonged to Charles X. Yellow gold filigree fans out from the center. It's what Frans's private jeweler called an estate piece. Something that could be handed down through generations. I only care if Samantha likes it. Her eyes glitter with joy as I slip it on her finger.

Her breasts press against my chest, and I struggle to focus on the sentiment of the moment. Definitely not the way her stomach rubs against my cock. Until she does it again. And again. "Very naughty," I say with a grunt.

A grin. "You did promise me something on the window."

"We don't need a window for that." I pull her up so that her knees straddle my face. I pull her hips down and make good on my promise. She gasps at the sudden switch. It's not two separate things, my love and my desire. They're like the emerald set in gold filigree, each part empty without the other. I use my tongue to make her moan—more, more, more. Until she's pressing her body down in urgent pulses. Until the rushes take her over. Moisture spills down my chin. *Christ.* She's wearing my ring. I should fuck her in a bed. Instead I flip her over so she's on her back, the thick carpet her only protection from marble floors. I push her legs wide. Next time we'll use a bed. For now I need to be inside. I plunge into her, savoring the wet heat, cursing my pleasure at the way she encases me. "My little prodigy. Mine."

Her head dips back, and I lick her neck in a

primal claim.

"Play me a chord."

To make sure she obeys me, I flick my thumb against her clit. She bucks against my body, trapped between my weight and the rug, the sound of her ecstasy sweet in my ear, the sexual strains the perfect counterpoint to the hard thrusts I use to find my end.

BETHANY

I STARE AT the door the way that Samantha stared at her violin, in silent challenge. It's a losing battle. It's nightfall when I finally stride across the room and turn the knob. The hallway seems to hold its breath. Complete silence. It sounds loud in my ears.

I'm sure Liam is comforting Samantha...

Actually, it's probably the other way around. He looked haunted when he pulled her out of that well. Romeo went in search of his handsome servant as soon as we got back. I'm sure the married couple who live here are together.

I'm one of the few people in one of these rooms alone. There's one other person I know I'll find by himself. The darkness peeking under his door gives me pause. What if he doesn't want me here? Of course he won't want me here.

A soft knock.

No answer. No sound of movement inside.

What if he's having complications? I know from my time in Cirque du Monde that hits on the head can always turn serious. He won't appreciate my concern, that's for sure. I push inside anyway. The tightness in my chest won't let me leave.

Pitch black.

My eyes slowly accommodate to the darkness. Sofas and side tables stand like sentinels. I creep past them to the bedroom door. Draperies in both rooms have been battened down against the moonlight. The shadows on the bed don't move, not even to breathe. They don't make any sounds, but I feel his presence anyway, his intense life force held in stasis.

As I step closer the shape of him emerges from the night. His arms and shoulders—bare. That probably means he's naked under the heavy blanket. His strong features in rare repose. A frown mars his forehead. It's the only sign of awareness. The only sign of life. Even his chest barely stirs with each exhale. I put my knee on his bed, which feels like a violation. Then I touch two fingers to his brow. A small caress between enemies. After a moment his expression smooths into that deep slumber.

I come from a family of superstitions. Joshua North would surely mock me if he knew about the voodoo and the tarot cards my mamere read. But he can't mock me now. The orange bottle on his nightstand shows the reason why. I doubt his usual reflexes would allow me to sneak up on him this way. He took pain medicine, which I can only imagine means he was in absolute agony. Otherwise he would resist it. He doesn't have his usual defenses, so I'll watch over him. I settle into a chair on the side of the room.

Superstitious or not, I'll keep the evil spirits away from him for tonight. I stay there until my shoulders become stiff. Until my right foot falls asleep. By the time the early sun peers between the slats in the drapes, I'm already gone. He never needs to know I was here.

CHAPTER TWENTY-ONE

LIAM

FOOTMEN CARRY OUR bags through the service exit while I lead Samantha down the broad staircase. Isabella and Bethany wait at the bottom to say goodbye. I leave them to their hugs and promises of texts. The doors to the library stand open, like sentries. Frans stands at his desk, reading something on a tablet, a frown marring his forehead. He looks up when I enter.

"Thank you for letting us use the jet," I say, crossing the room. North Security consulted on the safety and security of the aircraft, as we have for many of our wealthy clients. I've placed the necessary order to purchase our own, but it will be several months before it's fully outfitted. It became necessary now that our most famous client needs to travel for her musical appearances.

Frans accepts my handshake. "I don't think Isa and I will be traveling soon."

Probably not, considering the paparazzi

camped outside the chateau's gates. The ramped up security we put in place for Samantha's visit will remain until the furor dies down. Every newspaper features a photograph of a young woman masterfully playing a violin, along with headlines that proclaim *Conspiracy Uncovered* and *International Scandal.*

"Thank you also for bearing witness." Frans is as dangerous as any man on my payroll, but that's not the primary reason I brought him along two nights ago. It's his word that won't be questioned, even in the highest circles of the European governments. The aristocracy doesn't have the weight it used to, but some of the conventions are alive and well.

"Hell. I spend over two million a year on security. Not to mention the pomp and circumstance. If there wasn't some upside it would be unbearable."

"Considering my company accepts much of that two million, you could say I benefit from your title in multiple ways."

A low laugh. "The US government lost a brilliant strategist when they let you go."

I walk to the window and look out, crossing my arms. They didn't want to let me go. I was more than a strategist. I was an operator, an assassin. I was anything they needed me to be. A weapon made of flesh and bone. It was only Samantha who got me out. She felt like a responsibility to bear. Something I had to do out of guilt. Instead she's become my salvation.

"You're upset this isn't more resolved," Frans says, his voice low so the women still bubbling with friendly chatter and laughter don't hear him.

"There's more at stake than political corruption and the future of the world," I manage to say in a light tone. "Samantha won't be at peace until her father's actions are fully revealed."

"It takes longer than six months to take apart a conspiracy that's been decades in the making. And I wouldn't be so sure about Samantha not finding peace. The women. They're stronger than us that way. They make their own happiness."

"You sound like you speak from experience."

"I am a married man."

"For what? One month now." My amusement fades. "I do wish you well."

"And you, my friend." He puts the tablet in front of me. Buried off the front page is a small piece that describes how two men of unknown origin have been taken into custody. Officially, information is being withheld in the interests of national security. The article resorts to innuendo with surprising accuracy. The diplomatic community is in an uproar. Russia demands the release of the two men. The United States claims no knowledge of their activity. Security clearances everywhere are being evaluated, as it becomes common knowledge, if only in the intelligence community, that a massive conspiracy has been perpetrated. How high does it go? the article asks at the end.

Frans is right. I might wish it was completely resolved, but with roots this deep in the political landscape it will take time to pull them out. "In two weeks the statement we pulled from those men will be leaked to a US newspaper."

A pause. "Understood. I'll tell my contacts they have that much to get their house in order."

The important thing is that Samantha is safe. I leave the library to find her waiting for me on the front drive. Already the clouds have cleared. The events of that night are public knowledge in private circles. Reporters already connect her father's actions to the attempt on her life. They're digging through his travel dates. They're looking at his contacts. Rather than silencing Samantha, they're trying to distance themselves from the whole debacle now. It won't work. Already men who were interns and lackeys ten years ago are coming forward. Demanding immunity. They don't want anything to do with the old regime, and they're willing to sell out their former bosses to ensure that they won't be connected.

The important thing is that Samantha is safe, and that has to be enough for me. What did Frans say? That the women made their own happiness. Yes. That does describe her. Her eyes shine with relief and anticipation of a lifetime to come.

I'm helpless in the face of her hope. I always have been.

I lean down to press a kiss to her forehead. My eyes close—in relief and anticipation of a lifetime to come. My eyes close in hope. "Thank you," she murmurs, as if I saved her two nights ago. How did I ever think I could walk away from her? It wasn't a question of love. I loved her since I held her in my arms, her small body ravaged by poison.

It wasn't even a question of lust.

It was warfare, plain and simple. A war that I fought for as long and hard as my soldier's heart could bear. Like most wars, it wasn't lost in a single battle. There were losses along the way— following her in the apartment in Nantes, taking her to see the sights in Paris. Fucking her on the balcony. It died a little at every battle, the part of me so determined to be alone. As if that made me stronger.

She's the winner in combat, the warrior, the one to whom I wave the white flag.

Surrender. It's never seemed like a sign of strength until now.

SAMANTHA

DRIP. DRIP. DRIP.

The cold water seeps through my skin. It sinks into my bones. The blackness closes around me until it's hard to breathe. Panting fills the air around me. Mine. The faint slush of the water sounds painfully loud to my sensitive ears.

There's no relief. It's endless. Forever.

"Samantha."

Is that Liam? He seems far away. He won't know that I'm down here. If no one finds me I'll spend my last days in this pool of freezing water. I'll spend my last hours here.

"*Samantha.*"

Liam. I try to call out to him, but it feels like I'm paralyzed. I can't move my lips, my tongue. I can't make a single noise. What if he's too late? What if I'm already dead? He would find me lying here eventually. I know he wouldn't give up.

It would make him so sad. He would grieve me.

Suddenly I'm moving. Light blinds me. Shivering wracks my body. An explosion of sound like the roar of thunder. No, like a plane. The humming underneath my seat reminds me of where I am. I open my eyes to look directly into an intense green gaze.

"You're safe now," he says, his voice rough, as if he's been yelling.

Maybe he has been.

A nightmare. That's what it was. A nightmare that I was trapped underneath the Palais Garnier. It wasn't real, even though I feel chilled to my core. As if he understands that, Liam wraps his arms around me. He pulls me close until it's hard to know where he ends and I begin. "I'm sorry," I say, forcing the words out. The feeling of being paralyzed hasn't fully left.

A stewardess appears holding a blanket. He accepts it without a word, wrapping it around me. The plush warmth enfolds me. The rise and fall of his chest comforts me. His voice comes low and steady this time. "It may take some time for the dreams to stop."

I remember walking into his room at Kingston...

A form writhes on the bed, large, menacing. A wild sound of rage. Of pain?

"Liam?" I whisper.

My eyes adjust so slowly, revealing a feral animal, revealing a man in sleep. White sheets are tangled around his waist. His shoulders are thick with muscle. He grasps the sheets, the pillows, fighting something. My heart clenches at the realization.

Liam North is having a nightmare.

I put my hand on his shoulder. Tension ripples beneath my palm. He's facing down, fighting some invisible enemy, sweat a faint gleam across a landscape of strength.

He goes still.

"It's just a dream," I say, soothing. Only it doesn't feel like a dream. There are terrible demons in the room, as living and breathing as I stand here. Maybe more.

A crash of motion, and then I'm pulled, twisted, pinned onto the bed. I land hard on the expanse of cool sheets. Breath leaves me in a rush. A large body cages me from above, an arm pressed across my neck. It's not hard enough to keep me from breathing, but I definitely can't move.

"Liam," I say, gasping. "Liam!"

He trembles above me, around me. He's become my whole world—and it's a dark place to live. His breath saws through the air like a serrated blade.

"How dare you," he says, his voice guttural.

He's asleep, he's still asleep, and I don't know how to wake him up. Only then his hand moves from my neck to my jaw.

His thumb brushes over my cheek. "Samantha," he mutters.

"I'm sorry," I say, more for whatever horrors haunted him in the nightmare than for waking him. Someone should be here every night, to pull him back to the land of the living.

"I could have hurt you." He sounds hoarse but coming awake. "Do you have a goddamn death wish, Samantha? I could have killed you."

I'm trembling underneath him, still trying to make sense of how I ended up on his bed, how I ended up between his thighs, the heavy weight of something on my stomach. "You wouldn't hurt me," I say, the words coming breathless and unsure.

The smell of him—earth and musk and salt. It's all I can think about, the way he surrounds me. The way he moves over me. This is how it would feel if we made love. Even his arm across my neck... it's meant to be a violent act, but it feels sensual. My nerves pick apart every sensation: the heat of him, the rasp of hair across his forearm, the throb of his pulse.

This is every erotic dream I've ever had, every-thing I see when I close my eyes, my hands between *my legs. It would be perfect—if he wasn't still trembling from aftershocks. What kind of terrible thing would make Liam so scared he would lash out like an animal? He's the most controlled person I've ever met.*

He dips his head, his lips against the curve of my ear. "I would," he murmurs, but it sounds like he's trying to convince himself. "You aren't safe with me."

How far we've come from that night. I'm the one with the nightmares now. There's no one better to comfort me. No one who understands them better than this man.

"Yes," I whisper with certainty. "I'm safe now."

He holds me with quiet assurance. There are no words to make the memories go away. Only human touch will do that. The certainty that I'm alive. The knowledge that I'm not alone. "I love you, Samantha Brooks," he says, giving me the words I asked for on the train, proving that I'm wrong. There are words that make the memories fade away. They're a beautiful music, infused with truth. Spoken with an instrument as old as my Stradivarius. Written on paper as worn as the parchment from Debussy.

"I love you, too." It doesn't matter how many

stages I stand on. This is the performance of my life, speaking four simple words while I'm tucked in his arms.

CHAPTER TWENTY-TWO

SAMANTHA

HOW MANY AFTERNOONS have we worked this way?

I sit on a plain chair in the middle of an over-large music room, playing until my fingers turn red and bruised. Liam works quietly a few yards away, his office door open, the extensive grounds of North Security's training field through the window beyond him.

It's a peaceful existence, one that's about to become a lot more chaotic.

Time to let Liam in on that secret.

I set the bow to the strings and play a song I've never played before. It takes Liam a three-count before his head rises. A whole refrain before he gets up and crosses the room. He leans against the doorframe, arms crossed, a slight frown. "What's that?"

I can't help but laugh. "Don't you recognize it? You need to get online more."

The bow runs through the refrain again. It's a simple song, after all. Made for children to enjoy. *Baby shark, doo doo doo doo doo.* He has no idea. It's adorable. There's going to be a lot for him to learn, though ironically, he has more experience being a parent than me. We'll learn the rest of it together. "Baby makes three," I say softly.

He stares at me, dumbfounded. "No."

"I should have explained," I say, teasing. "About the birds and bees."

"Not this bird." He kneels in front of me, placing a hand on my still-flat stomach. There isn't fear in his eyes now. Only love. "Not this bee. Samantha, is it true?"

"It's true." My eyes fill with tears. They're ones of joy. Not pain.

He's made of muscle and scar tissue. A fortress of a human being, but he renders himself vulnerable for me. He rests his head in my lap, exposing his nape. I ruffle my fingers through his pale brown hair. This is how we make a family. Not with haunting memories but with music.

This is how we compose our future—one note at a time.

EPILOGUE

SAMANTHA

WATER LAPS AT my ankles, surprisingly cold on a warm day. A breeze whispers against wet skin. I compose a letter in my mind. *Dear mama.* No. *Dear mother.* Also no. *To whom it may concern, I'm getting married today.* I've lived long enough without actual relatives. I don't think about it all the time, but right now, there's a family-shaped hollow in my heart. Isn't this when they come together? A mother to help me dress. A father to walk me down the aisle. A church full of people to throw rice. There's no church. No aisle. There is a dress, although it doesn't have a train or a veil. White silk flutters in the wind, threatening at any moment to break from my grasp and get entirely wet.

I glance back. Liam stands at the edge of the water. A white dress shirt molds to his muscular frame, pushed by the wind into the dips between muscle. Black dress pants. Dress shoes, incongruous on a beach. There's no impatience in his frame. No movement. He might as well be made of stone, waiting for years for me to come back from sea, the personification of Penelope. Which would make me Odysseus, traveling for ages before I could finally come home.

You are my mother. I need you.

No.

I'm getting married today to a man I love. He's my anchor in the world. It's not right that I didn't have you as my anchor. It's not right that you left. I spent so many years looking for you, not in real places, in emotional places, in tender, heart-dark places. Liam has been waiting for me.

Yes. Finally, yes.

He waited for me to grow up. He waited for me to need him—not as a child but as a woman.

He's waiting for me now.

A wave crashes against my shins. I walk back toward the shore. Undercurrent wraps around my toes, urging me back into the water, but I don't want to go that way. Choices, choices. Green eyes glint in the bright sun. This is the home I choose. The family I found. This man.

He holds out his hand. "Ready?"

Emotion tightens my throat. It pricks my eyes. I take his hand without a word. He seems to know the feelings running through me. Shadows and light. Dark striations in a malachite gaze. I reach to cup his jaw. It's only six o'clock, but he already has a light scratch of hair. I stroke it, gently, against the grain, reveling in its sandpaper texture. "I'm ready."

His nostrils flare. There are more than words passing between us. There are animal instincts. *Are you my mate? Yes, yes, yes.* The low gravel of his voice rolls over my skin. "If you keep looking at me like that, there isn't going to be a ceremony."

An officiant waits beneath a driftwood arch. White silk and white roses hang down in artful flourish. Everything appeared with startling ease. The private resort does one wedding a day. They didn't appreciate having to clear their schedule for two weeks. Liam made it worth their while.

I lift up to press a kiss to his cheek. "Thank you."

He frowns. Gratitude still bothers him. I plan to shower him with it. Exposure therapy. Endless gratitude until it hurts less than torture, at least slightly. "You know you can have a different wedding. Another wedding. We can call Josh and—"

"That would be silly. Josh can't give me away."

"Elijah, then."

"He's almost my age."

"Frans offered. He also said we could use the chateau."

"Oh gosh, no. That would be a circus. Besides, it wouldn't change this moment. None of them can give me away. None of them own me." I brush my thumb over his lips. He has to bend down for me to reach him this way. I could pull with all my strength. It would be like tugging at the moon. He moves because he wants to, my own personal tide. "You own me."

"So I should walk you down the aisle—like a father."

"And you should marry me when we get to the end, like my lover."

He opens his mouth. Before I can move my hand away, he has my forefinger between his teeth. Biting down. Sucking gently. It's a warning and a privilege. "I should take you right here, push you on the sand, spread your legs apart, fuck you while the water swells around you."

My breath catches. "What would the priest think?"

"He would be jealous, of course. Any man would be. You look like a goddess in that dress, rising from the sea. You look untouchable.

Moonlight. I wouldn't fuck you like a goddess, though. Flesh and blood. Coming around my cock, your sex wet as the ocean around us."

"Liam," I whisper, urgent as I press my legs together.

I lean against him, my palms rubbing up his shirt. He's been strict about sleeping in his own room since we got to the resort. I chose the location and the flowers and the cake. He chose this. "You haven't been touching yourself, have you, little prodigy?"

My cheeks flame. "I'm sorry."

"I might have to punish you for that."

If I'm going to be punished anyway, I may as well explore him like I want to. My hand drifts down over the ridges of his abdomen. Over the flat plane. And the iron-hard bulge beneath his dress slacks. He grunts. That's his only reaction. No part of his body moves, even as I explore the shape of him through black wool. "Have you been touching yourself?"

"Of course. Every night I'm hard and hurting for you. Thinking of how pink you look, how sweet. I have to fuck my fist for relief, but that only makes it worse."

My heart thuds against my ribs. I'm feverish. "Then maybe I should punish you."

"You already do, little prodigy. Your beauty is my punishment. Your strength. It hurts enough that any sane man would have looked away." He gazes at me with unflinching honesty. "I love you, Samantha. For what it's worth, it's yours. Everything I have."

I press a kiss to his chest. Salt mixes with man. It fills my lungs. "Everything you have. Before the tour, before I left Kingston, before I grew into a woman, I might not have understood. I have your heart, but it's more than that, isn't it? I have your guilt and your desire and your hope."

"Yes," he says, his voice hoarse. "Everything."

"Do I have your forgiveness, too?"

"What?"

"Will you forgive me for the well?" I don't bother to specify which well. The well beneath the Palais Garnier. The well in his hellish childhood. Mostly I mean the well that lives inside his mind, the place he's kept himself for so many years. A mental prison—and also, perversely, a place to stay safe. Something recognizable. The opposite of the well isn't dry land. The water isn't the enemy. It's the endless expanse of the ocean. That's the opposite. Freedom instead of confinement.

Forgiveness instead of an eternity locked in the darkest place.

His expression turns hard. "You did nothing wrong."

"Then forgive *yourself* for the well, Liam. You did nothing wrong either."

He searches my eyes. "You're determined to heal me."

"I love you."

"How can you be so sure I'm wounded?"

He's always been this way, stoic so other predators wouldn't sense his weakness, hiding a mortal wound beneath layers of muscle and fur and willpower. "Haven't you ever wondered why you're so determined to protect me? It wasn't only because of responsibility or guilt. Not even only because of love. You were determined to protect me from the same hell you experienced."

"I thought I deserved it," he says, his voice breaking. "Even my brothers, even when I stood up for them, it seemed like we belonged in hell. Only when I saw you did I understand the horror of it. Only then did I know I'd die before letting you feel pain."

Breath expands my lungs. I'm bursting with gratitude and affection. And love. "There's no such thing as life without pain. It would mean there's no pleasure, either. You were Don Quixote, tilting at the windmills of an unattainable ideal. Complete happiness."

"Do you think I'll apologize for that? I'll drag heaven down for you."

Of course he would. He already has. It's not the brilliant blue water or the fine-grained white sand that makes paradise. It's the deep green of his eyes. I can drag heaven down for him, too, once we're alone. I know how. There's more to learn, but he lets me explore his body—and he doesn't hide his reactions. I can hear every intake of breath and every groan. At least until three days ago. "Forget the flowers. Forget the cake. Let's go back to the room."

A muscle works in his jaw. *Restraint.* "Not until we're married."

He offers his arm. There's a wealth of meaning in that one gesture—the promise of protection, of loyalty. The promise of forever. I rest my hand on his forearm, feeling the solidity of him, the warmth.

We walk down the beach in a straight line. It's a route not marked on any map. It's a path we make together, the notes written on the sand beneath our feet, the flourish added with the wind-whipped silk hem of my dress.

Liam walks me down the coastal aisle like a father would his daughter. Even his hand that rests on mine, holding me in place, reassuring me, carries the weight of guardianship. Only when we reach the end does he turn to face me. We stand both equal and opposite, a note and its counter-point—a man and a woman claiming our place side by side.

THANK YOU

Thank you for reading SONATA! I hope you absolutely loved Liam and Samantha's emotional and scorching story. You can read Josh and Bethany's emotional and incredibly sexy story... Order AUDITION right now!

And now the third and final North brother, Elijah, has a book...

I'm stepping off a nine-hour flight when it happens. A white van. A dark hood. Every woman's worst nightmare. Now I'm trapped in an abandoned church. The man who took me says I won't be hurt. The man in the cell next to me says that's a lie. I'll fight with every ounce of strength, but there are secrets in these walls. I'll need every single one of them to survive.

Sign up for the VIP Reader List to find out when I have a new book release:
www.skyewarren.com/newsletter

Join my Facebook group, Skye Warren's Dark Room, for exclusive giveaways and sneak peeks of future books. Turn the page for an excerpt...

EXCERPT FROM
DIAMOND IN THE ROUGH

THE AIRPORT FEELS sleepy, heavy shades drooping over dark windows. Workers push large floor cleaners across a floor that's lost its gloss. Every other restaurant has bars over its entrance. Closed. Good thing I'm not hungry.

It's four a.m. The embassy opens in a few hours.

A lone suitcase circles the conveyor belt. A family with two children appear with a large stuffed elephant that probably needed its own seat. A selection of individual men and women, probably business travelers. A couple who are leaning on each other. Honeymoon? We're all too exhausted to do anything more than stare straight ahead.

The man from the plane doesn't show up. Charles Bisset. I don't know whether I'm disappointed not to see him again. He would have made small talk, and I hate small talk.

Except when it's with handsome strangers, apparently.

Then even talking about the weather would make a little fire pitch inside my stomach.

He probably only brought a carry on. Except he hadn't pulled one down from the overhead bins. He'd only had a leather briefcase. Strange, even for someone traveling light.

A loud buzzing sound heralds the arrival of our luggage. They slide down the chute, stacking on each other in clumps like a poorly played game of Tetris. After a full revolution of the carousel, my purple bag appears. I grasp it and pull, almost falling backwards.

Signs lead the way through customs and border control. I'm snapped at in rapid French for not checking the right box on the form. And then I'm finally free to find the exit. A big blue sign proclaims TAXI. I pull my luggage along the rubbery floor, eager for a breath of fresh air. A block of exhaust envelopes me. The crowd of people shout and wave their arms, a stark contrast to the languor inside the airport. These aren't travelers. That registers first. They don't have luggage. They're wearing jackets and holding signs. Protestors. Something about Uber. A row of yellow and black taxis don't appear to be moving.

A group of men surround a black Escalade, pushing, pushing, and I let out a shriek that no one hears. A window breaks, and they cheer.

"They're on strike," comes a low voice behind me, and I gasp. Charles gives me an apologetic smile. "The taxi drivers. Only a matter of time before they get violent."

I watch them rock the Expedition back and forth on its wheels. "That's not violent?"

"More violent," he amends. "It'll be hell getting out of here"

Anxiety grips my chest. "What should I do?"

He pauses, seeming almost embarrassed. "You could get a train. Or… look, I hesitate to say this. I don't want you to think I'm hitting on you. Again, that is. But I have a towncar waiting. One fo those things you schedule before the trip. They wait in a different lane than taxis."

Relief is a steaming cup of coffee on a terrible morning. "God, that sounds—no, I couldn't. I mean it sounds wonderful, but I couldn't inconvenience you that way."

He nods, once. Then turns, as if to walk away. Then looks back. "Where are you going? It might be on the way to where I'm going. Maybe."

Hope sparks inside me. "The embassy. The American embassy."

A pause. He rubs a large palm across his jaw, and I can hear the scrape of his growth from here. "I believe that's in central Paris. Where I'm heading. Listen, are you in some kind of trouble? We could look for a cop around here. I'm sure we can find one."

That's what decides me, that genuine note of concern in his voice. "No, I'm not in trouble. It's my sister. She's been missing a week already. I have to go to the embassy."

His brown eyes soften. "I can get you to central Paris. Then you can grab a cab."

"Thank you. God." A stone smashes a window. "So much."

He takes the handle of my suitcase before I can object. Then he's wheeling it over a bumpy sidewalk crossing. I struggle to keep up with his long strides. We round a corner, and everything becomes suddenly quiet. It's almost eerie, the way sound doesn't travel around this building. As if the riot a few yards away was a dream.

There's not a neat row of black towncars. There's only a lonely road. And a dumpster.

I do a little skip to eat up the pavement. "Are you sure this is the right way?"

"I'm sure," he calls back, not slowing for an instant.

Nervous energy hits my body like I've run into a wall. Sparks in my ches. A thud at the base of my skull. I suck in air through a straw. I can't trust him, this Charles Bisset. That might not even be his name. My step falters, but he has my suitcase. All my things. My clothes. Pictures of my sister. Her birth certificate. What if I take it from him? What if I rip it out of his hand and run back to the cabs? Part of me feels ridiculous for even thinking it. He's done nothing wrong. All he did was walk fast. That's not a crime. Twenty four years of social conditioning tell me to act normal. Act nice. The persistent rat-tat-tat of my heart warns me that something is wrong.

"Excuse me? Mr. Bisset. *Charles.* Wait."

He doesn't wait. He just keeps walking, and that's when I know, when I *know*, that I'm in trouble. I stop mid-step. I need what's in the suitcase. How can I make my way in a foreign city without clothes? But I can't follow this man into—where? I take a step back.

The screech of a tire snaps me to attention. A white van bumps onto the curb. The man inside wears a black ski mask. Time slows to a crawl. Gravel sprays from the thick black tires. The protestors dim to a low roar. *They won't hear me if I scream.* I turn toward Charles, as if he might protect me. And for a moment, he does. He pulls me close to him, shielding me. He murmurs in my ear, "Don't fight, mon cherie. It will only make this harder for you.'"

My eyes widen. Then something black and thick covers my head. Hands drag me toward the van, and I fight, blind and in shock, lashing out at nothing before my arms are caught behind my back. Then I'm shoved roughly into something in motion. Something hard hits my face. The floor. I'm slammed to the side. A sharp pain behind my head. And then darkness.

✧   ✧   ✧

MY EYES OPEN to pitch black.

I wait for my bedroom to come into focus. Nothing happens. This is the complete kind of darkness, the kind without even shadows. My lungs burn, as if I've been holding my breath. I gulp down damp and moldy air. I curl my fingers against stone. Faintly slick. Biting cold.

Where am I?

Memories drop into my mind like rain in a puddle. I remember the long flight and fear for my sister. I remember the man with the movie star smile.

A shudder works its way through my body,

lingering in aches and bruises, waking up pain as it goes. I move myself to a sitting position with a soft groan. The floor feels slightly uneven, almost like a natural rock formation. A cave or something.

I crawl forward. Something hard meets my face. My fists close around iron bars.

Not completely natural, then.

Charles Bisset. *Shar-el.* Why did he take me? Because I'm a tourist? Maybe he thought I'd have money. That's no reason to take me, only my bags.

Or maybe he recognized me as the famous children's book author. Except that the only person who could pay ransom is my sister, and she's missing.

There's no other reason he would take me.

Isn't there? The soft voice inside my head knows exactly why a man would take a woman. He asked me out, didn't he? He asked to show me around the city. I said no.

He doesn't take rejection well.

The darkness closes in on me, it becomes a tactile force, squeezing my lungs. I don't want to stay here, in this pitch black prison. I *can't* stay here. There's no oxygen. I gasp through the fist around my throat. I'm going to die here, before

Charles can even touch me, and that seems almost like a gift, except that the body fights anyway. It wants to live.

"Easy," comes a voice from the inky void. I choke on air. "Easy there," he says again.

"Charles," I gasp out. It's twisted that I'd actually be relieved to have him here. Anything is better than being alone right now. Even the presence of my captor.

There's quiet.

I'm not alone in the dark, though. My fists curl around iron. "Answer me."

"I'm not Charles." And he's not. He's missing the fluid accent. He says the name the American way, with harsh syllables. His voice is completely different—lower, more blunt, gravelly like the broken concrete underneath me.

"Who are you?" Was he the driver of the van? Or someone else?

"I'm no one." Shadows curl around his rough voice. His presence settles into my skin, deeper than the dust, farther than the cold. He's someone, this stranger.

Want to read more? DIAMOND IN THE ROUGH is available on Amazon, iBooks, Barnes & Noble, Kobo, and other book retailers!

Books by Skye Warren

Endgame trilogy & more books in Tanglewood

The Pawn

The Knight

The Castle

The King

The Queen

Escort

Survival of the Richest

The Evolution of Man

A Modern Fairy Tale Duet

Beauty and the Professor

Falling for the Beast

Chicago Underground series

Rough

Hard

Fierce

Wild

Dirty

Secret

Sweet

Deep

Stripped series

Tough Love

Love the Way You Lie

Better When It Hurts

Even Better

Pretty When You Cry

Caught for Christmas

Hold You Against Me

To the Ends of the Earth

For a complete listing of Skye Warren books, visit

www.skyewarren.com/books

About the Author

Skye Warren is the New York Times bestselling author of dangerous romance such as the Endgame trilogy. Her books have been featured in Jezebel, Buzzfeed, USA Today Happily Ever After, Glamour, and Elle Magazine. She makes her home in Texas with her loving family, sweet dogs, and evil cat.

Sign up for Skye's newsletter:
www.skyewarren.com/newsletter

Like Skye Warren on Facebook:
facebook.com/skyewarren

Join Skye Warren's Dark Room reader group:
skyewarren.com/darkroom

Follow Skye Warren on Instagram:
instagram.com/skyewarrenbooks

Visit Skye's website for her current booklist:
www.skyewarren.com

COPYRIGHT

This is a work of fiction. Any resemblance to actual persons, living or dead, business establishments, events or locales is entirely coincidental. All rights reserved. Except for use in a review, the reproduction or use of this work in any part is forbidden without the express written permission of the author.